CHU JU'S HOUSE

Also by GLORIA WHELAN

THE IMPOSSIBLE JOURNEY

FRUITLANDS

ANGEL ON THE SQUARE

HOMELESS BIRD

MIRANDA'S LAST STAND

INDIAN SCHOOL

The Island Trilogy:

ONCE ON THIS ISLAND

FAREWELL TO THE ISLAND

RETURN TO THE ISLAND

CHU JU'S HOUSE

GLORIA WHELAN

HARPERCOLLINS*Publishers*

Chu Ju's House

Copyright © 2004 by Gloria Whelan

Library of Congress Cataloging-in-Publication Data
Whelan, Gloria.

   Chu Ju's house / by Gloria Whelan.—1st ed.

     p.   cm.

   Summary: In order to save her baby sister, fourteen-year-old Chu
Ju leaves her rural home in modern China and earns food and shelter by working on a fishing boat, tending silk worms, and planting
rice seedlings, while wondering if she will ever see her family again.

   ISBN 0-06-050724-1 — ISBN 0-06-050725-X (lib. bdg.)

   1. China—History—1976—Juvenile fiction. [1. China—History—
1976—Fiction. 2. Runaways—Fiction. 3. Sex role—Fiction.] I. Title.
PZ7.W5718Ch 2004   2003006979
[Fic]—dc21   CIP
                                                AC

Typography by Alison Donalty

1 2 3 4 5 6 7 8 9 10

First Edition

To Jeanine and Peter

one

It was the fifth day of the fourth moon, Tomb Sweeping Day, which some call the Day of Pure Brightness. It was just such a day, for the spring sky was bright blue and the fields of ripened winter wheat shone gold in the sun. All across the hills you could see villagers like ourselves making their way to their ancestors' graves.

I ran ahead on the goat path, happy to leave the village where it was all houses and people. The sweet smell of wild roses followed us up and down the hills. I loved the upness and downness of the hills. On this day I thought hills were the best idea of all.

"Chu Ju," my grandmother called, "you are like a wild dog let loose. Have a little dignity."

Nothing I did pleased my nai nai. I slowed my steps, as was proper for so solemn an occasion. We would ask of our ancestors the thing we had asked in the village of the palm reader and of the astrologer. It was the thing that was talked of in our home day and night, sometimes in whispers, sometimes in angry shouts. Often Nai Nai would look sharply at me as if it were all my fault, and often I felt it was.

We passed a small house where azalea bushes grew beside a pigpen. I took Ma Ma's hand and pointed out the pink piglets rooting among the pink blossoms. Ma Ma stood beside me smiling. The baby was due any time, and I guessed she was happy to rest for a moment.

Ba Ba paused to admire some rows of new corn. My father was a doctor, but his parents had been farmers and he had been a farmer until the government had taken their land and joined it with other farms to make a big farm. When his parents protested, they were punished and sent away to this place where we now live. Ba Ba had only been a small child then, but he remembered the farm and took great pleasure in anything that grew. That is a thing I have from Ba Ba.

"It is a good year for the corn," he said. He grinned at me. "Your little pigs will grow fat."

Below us the houses became small. The river, the Gan Jiang, curled around the village like a silver ribbon. Overhead soared a great *ying*, with its dark wings and white breast.

At last we came to the place where our ancestors were buried. The graveyard was small, with only three tombs. Ba Ba had planted a pear tree beside each tomb. The white pear blossoms drifted down like snowflakes, covering the graves. A little bird with an orange head peered at us from the top of one of the trees. Its song was like the *gu zheng*, the lyre, with its sweet sound.

During the years of war and revolution the people of China had been blown about like autumn leaves, settling now here, now there. With many tears they had left the graves of their ancestors. Few people could afford a trip of a thousand kilometers to return to those tombs. Nai Nai said it was the disgrace of all those untended graves that caused our country so much sorrow.

I had come to this resting place of our ancestors many times and knew the names on the stones by heart. I had seen the places set aside for my nai nai and my ma ma and ba ba and for a son if there should be one. I was saddened that there was no place for me. One day I would marry, and when I died I would lie with my husband in some distant place.

I was seven when Ye Ye died. I came with Ba Ba to find a suitable location for my grandfather's grave. Ba Ba brought with him his bamboo divination blocks, which would help him discover the most auspicious place, the place with the best *feng shui*. If your ancestors were displeased with their burial place, they could be mischievous and cause you trouble. Nai Nai had been unhappy with the site Ba Ba had chosen for her husband, but then Nai Nai was unhappy about everything.

Unlike Nai Nai, who could only see that I was not a son, Ye Ye had been kind to me and would pick the bits of meat from his rice and put them in my dish. When Ye Ye became sick, my ba ba prescribed a certain kind of snake for him and Ye Ye gave me bits of that cooked snake. For days I thought I felt it slithering about in my stomach.

As a special treat Ye Ye would take me with him to fish in the river. First we would catch grasshoppers for bait. Once I caught a cricket, but Ye Ye shook his head.

"Not a cricket," he said. "At night the crickets sing away the darkness." He wove a small bamboo cage for the cricket and put it beside my bed. "Now you will have only pleasant dreams," he promised.

We sat by the river, Ye Ye with his long bamboo pole and I with my small one. Together we would watch the barges make their way down the river. "There is no end to where the river can take you and no end to the wonders it can show you," Ye Ye said. "The river is not like a road that comes to an end. It goes to the great river, the Chang Jiang, and from there to the sea, the *hai*, and from there to another *hai*."

Ye Ye became silent, and I saw that he was on the river and floating toward the *hai* and from one *hai* to the next and from one wonder to an even greater wonder.

Once we saw a dead man strapped onto a raft floating down the river. I cried out, but Ye Ye said, "It is nothing more than a death custom that some practice. It is not for me, for I must be buried in the place my son will choose, but I would not think it a bad thing to travel forever on the river."

Often we talked with the fishermen who lived on the fishing boats with their families. A part of each boat was open. The other part had walls of bamboo mats and a roof of thatched paddy straw to make a small house. A stove for cooking stood in the open part of the boat. Tied to one side of the fishing boat was a smaller boat that held the nets for fishing. Each morning the fishermen would pole their small boats to favorable parts of the river for fishing. In the afternoon the whole family, even the young children, would carry the fish to the market. When the fish were sold, the family would pull up their anchor and move on. Like Ye Ye I dreamed of what it would be like to live on the river with no school and every day another village.

We mourned for many days after Ye Ye died, with much crying and wailing as was proper. I had not seen the death of someone I loved before, and all the time Ye Ye lay in his closed coffin, I worried about his being hungry. Finally the diviner gave us an auspicious day for the burial. There was a procession to the grave and Ye Ye was buried. Ma Ma assured me that he was now in a lovely country where he could fish as much as he liked, and that he would watch over us.

On this Tomb Sweeping Day, when we finally reached the graveyard, Nai Nai went at once to Ye Ye's grave and kowtowed, bowing her head to the ground and speaking words of greeting to her husband. She placed red candles by all the tombs, carefully lighting each candle, sheltering the matches from the spring breeze with her hand.

Ba Ba took a packet of gilt paper money and,

making a small golden pile, burned it. It was not real money but ghost money, money for our ancestors' use. Each piece of paper said THE BANK OF HEAVEN.

A school friend of mine once showed me bowls of noodles, a golden fish, and even an automobile, all made of paper. When I asked Ba Ba why we did not send food and automobiles to our ancestors, he shook his head and said, as he said to many things I suggested, "Not traditional." So all our ancestors got was money. I comforted myself with the thought that with so much money, they could buy whatever they wished.

As the money burned, we knelt down and kowtowed, asking of the ancestors the favor that was in all our hearts.

Ma Ma whispered, "Let the child be a healthy boy."

I echoed Ma Ma's wish: "Make the baby be a little brother."

In a solemn voice Ba Ba said, "Give us a son to

bring honor to our family."

In so loud a voice I was sure her words carried over the hills, Nai Nai said, "Send us a boy to care for us in our old age and not another worthless girl."

I, Chu Ju, was that worthless girl. Nai Nai's harsh words made my eyes sting with tears. All my joy in the hills and the spring day disappeared. I told myself that this asking favors of our ancestors was foolish superstition. In school we learned praying to our ancestors was old world. When we wished for something, we must look to the Communist Party, not to our ancestors. There was a poster in our schoolroom that said: THE PARTY IS YOUR BA BA AND YOUR MA MA. Even so I did not see how the Communist Party could give my parents a son.

The government said our country had too many mouths to feed. It was the patriotic duty of a family to have no more than one child if the family lived in a city, and no more than two children if the family lived in the country, where workers were needed in the fields and the rice paddies. Once their second baby was born, my parents would never be able to have another child. That meant that if the baby was a girl, there would be no further chance for a son.

If you were very rich, you might be able to have a third child by paying a huge fine, but our family had no money. My ba ba was only a barefoot doctor. During the Cultural Revolution anyone with an education was denounced and punished as an enemy of the people. All the teachers and doctors were sent to work as peasants in the fields. Many of them starved and perished. After the Cultural Revolution was over, there were not enough doctors to care for sick people.

Poor farmers like my ba ba were taken from the fields, and after six months' education in medicine they were sent into villages to become doctors. Such doctors were called barefoot doctors because they were supposed to be like the peasants, who went out barefoot into their fields to preserve their shoes.

While my ba ba was not a learned man, he was a kindly man. He could perform acupuncture so gently, you did not feel the needles being stuck into you and wiggled around. He wore a white coat, and in his shop he had glass jars with snakes and toads and a chart of a man showing all the three hundred and sixty-five sensitive points for the needles.

My nai nai knew where to gather healing herbs and how to use them. She had taught my ba ba these skills, so if you were sick he could do both needles and herbs. For his work my ba ba was often paid with a bag of rice or a hen or not paid at all. Certainly there was no money for fines for an extra child.

All that could be done to ensure a son had been done. Nai Nai gathered favorable herbs and made special teas for Ma Ma. Ma Ma had taken her own birth date to the astrologer in the village. He was a very old man who seemed reluctant to answer questions, as if his knowledge were money he had no wish to give away. He shrugged his shoulders and shook his head and only mumbled a few words, so there was no knowing for sure what would happen.

The palm reader was very different, exclaiming loudly over Ma Ma's hand and assuring her that she would indeed have a son. The palm reader had so much to say, and said it so loudly, that when she had finished, we could not believe her. While the astrologer gave away very little, the palm reader gave so much away that it seemed of little value. Our last hope lay in these prayers to our ancestors.

As we returned to the village from the graves, I lagged behind. My nai nai's words had spoiled the journey home, which now seemed to take forever. The sun was hot, and I had already drunk the jar of boiled water Ma Ma had brought for me. The hills were only wearying. Ma Ma stopped often to rest, and I sat beside her while Ba Ba and Nai Nai went on walking slowly so that we could catch up to them.

"Do not take Nai Nai's words to heart," Ma Ma said. "You are precious to me. If there should be a son, you will still be precious."

"Ma Ma, what will happen if the baby is a girl?"

Ma Ma's face clouded over. She looked to be sure that Nai Nai and Ba Ba were far enough ahead so that they could not hear. When she saw that Nai Nai was busy picking mushrooms, Ma Ma whispered, "I hope that we may keep the baby."

"Keep the baby?" I said, shocked. "What do you mean?"

As if she had eyes in the back of her head and could see us whispering together, Nai Nai called to us to join them. Ma Ma did not answer my question but only motioned me to help her up.

When we returned to the village, we found it crowded with people celebrating the festival day. In the Pleasant Hours Teahouse the men, seated in bamboo chairs, were busy with their games of *majiang*. I loved to peer over their shoulders at the tiles with their pictures of flowers. The tiles for the four winds had no pictures, only characters, which was suitable, for you cannot see the winds. There were no pictures for the red and white dragons either, so in my mind the dragons were always more frightening than any picture could make them.

One of the men at the teahouse had a birdcage with a mynah bird. The man had placed the cage on the table beside him so that the bird might enjoy the spring day. Every few minutes the bird squawked a bit and then said, *Go home, go home,* at which all the men would laugh.

Carts humped along over the cobbled streets. The market stalls were doing a good business. One shop sold slippers, another noodles, still another secondhand blue jeans. I looked hungrily at the jeans, but I was not allowed to have a pair. "Too costly," Nai Nai said. "Not traditional," Ba Ba said. Strung across the butcher's stall was a dripping necklace of roasted ducks. At the fishmonger's a red carp, newly caught, beat its tail against the counter. At one of the shop windows you could watch opera or soccer on the screen of a *dian-shi*.

We left Ba Ba at his stall, where there were patients waiting for him. I squinched my eyes shut as we passed the dentist who had the stall next to Ba Ba's shop. The dentist was trying to pull an old woman's tooth, but the woman kept instructing the dentist on how to do his job, refusing to be silent long enough to allow him to pull it out.

Our house at the edge of the village was made of stone. The stone made the house cool in the summer, but it was always damp, so bits of moss clung to the walls and the floors were cold on bare feet. There were two rooms, the room my parents slept in and the large room where we lived and where Nai Nai and I slept. There was a small ancestral altar, where Nai Nai burned an incense that stung my nose and made me sneeze. Next to the altar was a calendar given out by the state. There was a slogan for each month. This month the slogan was HELP CHINA TO BECOME EVER GREATER. Outside in our courtyard were a table and chairs, a stove for cooking, and the threshing stone.

No sooner had we reached the courtyard than Ma Ma sank down onto a chair. Her face was white, and I saw she was biting her lip. Nai Nai looked at her, then ordered, "Chu Ju, go at once for the midwife and then tell your ba ba your ma ma's time has come."

I looked at Ma Ma, who nodded her head. In a moment I was flying through the village streets. Soon I would have a little brother, for I was sure our ancestors would not disappoint us.

two

When I returned with Auntie Tai and Ba Ba, I was sent from the house and told to remain out of the way. As I left, I heard Ba Ba say to Auntie Tai, "This one must be a boy who will grow into a clever man, a man who could put his hand on a bit of land here and there. He would not be satisfied with our pitiful plot."

To make the time pass, I went to our pitiful plot and began to weed among the rows of garlic and onion. As always I kept a wary eye on the scarecrow. It was an ugly scarecrow, and it never ceased to frighten me. Bees buzzed in and out of the bean blossoms. I knew that Ba Ba would be happy to see how the cucumber vines were climbing their poles. I crept along the rows tugging at the weeds. Some came away in my hand lightly, others had roots that seemed to reach down to the very center of the earth. The smell of garlic and onion was on my hands. All the time I tugged at the weeds, I thought of my new brother, hoping that after he was born my nai nai and ba ba would stop looking at me as if I had done something wrong when it was not my fault that I was a girl.

Hours went by, but I heard nothing of a little brother. A soft rain began to fall. At first it was only a gentle touch on my cheek and hands, but soon I was pelted by large drops. A flock of bright-blue birds with black faces darted into the shelter of a camphor tree. I crouched under the eaves of our roof, not daring to go inside the house until I was called. Because of the importance of what was happening, I had been forgotten. If it is a little brother,

I thought, this is how it will be. They will forget about me, but that would be far better than having a sister and bearing Nai Nai's anger and Ba Ba's disappointment.

The courtyard filled with water. I took off my shoes to keep them dry. The stones under my feet were cold but the rain was warm. I could feel the vegetables' happiness at the rain. I thought the rain that made the crops grow was a good omen. I felt sure the baby would be a boy.

"Chu Ju," Nai Nai shouted. "Why are you crouching out there in the rain? Don't you have the sense to come into the house? You are needed at once. Make tea for Auntie Tai. There is much to do here."

My heart dropped into the pit of my stomach. If Nai Nai had been pleased with the baby, she would surely have made the tea for Auntie Tai. That the task should be left to a young girl was an insult to Auntie Tai.

In an offended voice Auntie Tai said, "I will not stop for tea. They will be expecting me at my next house, where they are sure to have my tea waiting for me and sesame cakes as well." There was no courteous *zai-jian* as she left.

"Since you have brought us a girl," Nai Nai called after her, "you would do well to find a place for her."

I crept into the small room in which my parents slept. Ma Ma was lying very still. Ba Ba was standing beside her looking down at a small bundle wrapped round and round with a cloth. There was deep disappointment on his face, but also a kind of wonder, the same look I had seen when he had gazed fondly at the green shoots in the cornfield. It was not a son, but it had lain like a tiny seed inside of Ma Ma, and it had grown and now here it was.

Nai Nai saw the look as well and said in a brisk voice to Ba Ba, "Your patients will be waiting for you at your shop. You had better see to them. You are only in the way here."

Ba Ba reached down to touch the bundle but seemed to think better of it.

As Ba Ba started for the door, Ma Ma pleaded, "You will have nothing done with the child?"

"The sooner something is done, the better," Nai Nai answered. "Are you to nurse and take care of her all day? You will get used to the child, and then what?"

In a weak voice Ma Ma said, "Two girls are not the greatest evil that could befall us. Chu Ju is a good worker."

Nai Nai said, "How long will that last? She will marry, and you will never see her again."

"She is just fourteen," Ma Ma said. "By the time she marries, her little sister will be there to help. Perhaps by then we will have a son."

"Talk of another child is foolishness," Ba Ba

said. "Some village tattletale would report to the government that we have three children, and the government would fine us so many yuan. We would have to sell everything we have to pay the fine. Or worse. You know that the officials knocked down Li's house because he had a third child. You cannot have a son to carry on our family name until this girl baby is gone."

Ba Ba's voice became less impatient. "We will wait a little," he said.

There were tears running down Ma Ma's cheeks. Nai Nai thrust the baby into my arms. "See to her. Let your ma ma sleep."

Here was this bundle in my arms. It was no heavier than a sack of rice or a melon. I did not know whether to hold the bundle tightly so that nothing should happen to it, or loosely so that something so tender would not be crushed.

I carried my sister into the other room and sat

down upon a chair and peered at her. She looked small and helpless, like a fledgling that falls from a bird's nest. She opened her eyes and I saw she was no fledgling bird, for there was nothing helpless in her eyes. They were shiny and black and crackled with life. She made little sucking sounds with her mouth and waved her tiny hands about. She was like a seedling that pushes up from the ground, bending this way and that until it gains more growth and can stand firm against the wind.

The baby began to whimper. I smoothed down the cap of black hair that stood straight up on her head. I walked back and forth holding the bundle and speaking to it in whispers, telling it that Ba Ba had said, "We will wait a little," so that there was no cause for whimpering.

From that moment, except for the times Ma Ma nursed her, the baby's care was given over to me. I remembered Nai Nai saying to Ma Ma, "You will get used to the child, and then what?"

After a few days I asked, "What will you name her?"

Nai Nai said, "There is no need for a name."

I trembled at Nai Nai's words, for I knew if the baby had a name, it would place her a little more firmly in our family. In my head I named her Hua, Blossom, because she was born on the day the beans blossomed and their fragrance was sweet on the air.

The days went by and Hua was still there. She was with me always. Nai Nai taught me how to wind a length of cloth to hold the baby on my back. When I went on an errand into the village she was with me. She slept beside me at night. Even if I was fast asleep, her softest cry awakened me. When I picked her up, the crying ceased. I was the first to hear the cooing noises she made like the call of the turtledoves that perched on the roof of our house.

At first her eyes were like shining black pebbles rolling about. After a bit they settled first on one thing and then another. Often the black pebbles fastened on my face, looking and looking until I wondered what Hua saw, for my face was only a plain face.

I thought of this baby like a puppy to be carried about with me, something to hold close to me and warm me and amuse me with her little tricks, a new one each day. Her smiles when they came were all for me.

But there was much work to be done for the little creature. I was awakened at night by Hua's cries and had to carry her to Ma Ma to be nursed. Again, early in the morning, I was awakened. All day long she had to be changed and cleaned. Sometimes there would be crying and I could find no reason for it. There was never a minute when I could wander to the village and spend time with a friend. So when Nai Nai argued day and night that something must be done with the baby, there were times when I did not care if my sister was sent away.

One day I was hoeing a row of turnips in our pitiful plot. The day was hot, and though I had put Hua in the shade of the chestnut tree, she whined with the heat. I was thirsty and sick of the whining. I left Hua in her basket and went to the house for boiled water, in no hurry to get back to my work and Hua's whining. I had drunk my water and was returning to take up the hoe when I saw a great black vulture settle on a branch of the chestnut tree just over Hua's basket. It had an ugly bald head, a cruel yellow beak, and sharp talons. I ran at it screaming and threatening it with the hoe. Such vultures stole ducks and piglets and even grown dogs. What might it have done to Hua?

My hands were shaking and my breath would not come. I sobbed with fright. Suppose through my fault I had let the vulture carry off my sister? After that everything changed. I would not let Hua out of my sight. When Nai Nai talked of how Hua must be sent away, how someone would come and take her, then Nai Nai became the vulture, ugly and cruel, and I hated her. When there was such talk, I held my sister close to me and hid with her in the fields.

As the weeks went by and Hua grew, she fretted and seemed hungry after her nursing. I begged a little rice gruel for her.

Nai Nai shook her head. "The milk is plenty. We have hardly enough rice for our own bowls."

When Nai Nai was not looking, I put a little of my rice aside to give to Hua and there was less crying.

Ma Ma held Hua tenderly after the nursing was over, and Ba Ba smiled when Hua's tiny hand curled around his finger, so I had a small hope that we might keep her after all, but one evening I found out that there was to be no keeping of Hua.

We were all sitting together finishing our rice mixed with a bit of dried fish. Ba Ba announced, "A woman will come tomorrow to make arrangements for the taking of the girl baby."

In her soft voice Ma Ma begged, "Let us keep her. She is already a part of us. What will become of her if we send her away?"

"That is not our worry," Nai Nai said. "There are orphanages for such children."

I looked at Ba Ba, but he only got up and left the house. Later in the evening, when he returned, I heard Ma Ma's voice and Ba Ba's voice long into the night.

I hardly slept for watching over Hua. The next morning, after Ba Ba left the house, the woman came. She was a big woman with small eyes, a tight mouth, and a mole on her cheek with a long black hair. She wore a large loose-fitting shirt and trousers and a shawl wrapped about her shoulders. I thought she could snatch Hua and hide her in all that cloth.

The woman looked closely at Hua as if she were counting her fingers and toes to see if they were all there. I was sure she had not noticed how bright Hua's eyes were or how neat and clean I kept her.

"An unremarkable girl baby," she said. "It will be difficult to find a place for her."

She named a price, and Nai Nai, who had never bothered to look at Hua, now began to point out her fine complexion, her thick hair, and her strong limbs. "Just see how she looks about and notices everything around her," Nai Nai said. "We are insulted by such a price. Twice the amount would be too little."

Hua gurgled and smiled at the horrible woman.

When the woman and Nai Nai were busy with their haggling and not looking at Hua, I reached slyly under Hua's shirt and pinched her hard. Immediately she began crying. I hoped the woman would not want a crying child.

"There," the woman said. "You are trying to sell me an ill-natured girl who will give everyone trouble."

I held my breath, hoping that the woman would not take her.

Nai Nai scowled at Hua. "She cries because she is insulted that you hold her so cheaply."

All the while Ma Ma sat in a corner of the room, pale and silent. As the two women argued, Ma Ma began to cry. I had wondered why Nai Nai had not sent her into the other room. Now I understood, for Nai Nai said, "We will not sell her after all. See, her ma ma is not willing to let her go." And indeed, Ma Ma was sobbing harder than ever; the sobs were not just show for the woman, but from Ma Ma's heart.

At this the woman offered more, for she could see that what Nai Nai said was true, that Ma Ma did not wish to part with Hua. What the woman did not understand was that Ma Ma had nothing to say in the matter.

At last a price was agreed upon, and the woman said she would make inquiries as to where Hua was to be taken and return for Hua the following morning.

Our meal that night was a silent one. Neither Ma Ma nor I could eat. Ba Ba kept his head down. Even Nai Nai held her tongue. When dinner was over and I had washed the bowls and scrubbed the wok, I took Hua out into the fields.

The spring evening was as pleasant as the house had been bitter. The summer sky still held the light of day. The ripe guavas hung on the trees like unlit lanterns. There was a light wind that made the scarecrow's shirtsleeves and trousers flutter. For a moment I feared it was moving toward me.

I clung more tightly to Hua. I had heard stories in the village of babies being carried off and never seen again. In any village there will be stories to make a little excitement and send tongues wagging. I had thought such stories were only meant to scare us in a delicious way.

Now I knew the stories of the babies being carried away were true. I looked down at Hua. She was asleep. Her long black eyelashes were a dark fringe on her cheeks. Her round pink mouth was a little open. Hua would be sent away so that the authorities would think our family had no more than one child. One day Ma Ma might have a son to please my nai nai and my ba ba.

If my ma ma could not stop Hua from being sent away, how could I? I wished I could disappear so that there would be only one daughter. The word *disappear* sounded in my head like the tiny insects you hear but cannot see. *Disappear, disappear*, they buzzed. *Then there will be just one child, Hua.*

But I was not a magician. I could not make myself disappear. *Think of the map*, the tiny insects buzzed. The map had stretched all the way across the wall of our schoolroom. The whole wall was China. At the bottom of the map was a scale that told how many kilometers the millimeters stood for. The length of my little finger was many kilometers on the map. You could travel thousands of kilometers and still be in China.

When I was little, to escape my nai nai's scolding I had hidden in the branches of a nearby banyan tree. If I tucked my legs under me and kept still, she could not find me. If I could hide so close to our house, why couldn't I hide somewhere in the great map?

At first I was pleased with the idea of disappearing. I thought of the excitement of starting out on such a journey. I thought of the wonders of China we had studied in school—the great wall in the north and the huge cities where many of the houses had a *dian-shi* and around every corner was a cinema.

There were factories in the cities. Perhaps I could get a job, for I knew how to make silk flowers. In our village school our teacher had handed out silk petals to the children along with strands of wire and green tape. All week we worked at making silk flowers, arranging the petals, fastening them with a bit of glue and sticking them on the wire we had wrapped with the green tape. We made blue flowers and pink flowers and red flowers, flowers such as I had never seen. The teacher said such flowers would be sold in distant countries, and the money they brought would help our school.

When he heard of the flower making, my ba ba complained that instead of studying, our time in class was taken up in making flowers for the school to sell; but the people at the school said such money was needed, for the school didn't have enough desks and there was no blackboard, only the wall that had been covered with thick black paint. Some whispered that we were lucky. In one school the children had made fireworks. There was a dreadful explosion and the whole school blew up with many children killed. There could be no explosion with silk flowers.

Why could I not disappear in a city, where I could make silk flowers and have a *dian-shi*, wear jeans, and go to the cinema? I thought again of the map and how far away such cities were. I remembered young men from our village who had gone to those cities and been sent to jail, for they went with no government permission and no proper government papers. I had heard stories—told in hushed voices by the village women—of young girls who traveled to the cities and were never heard from again. I did not think I would go to the city, even for a *dian-shi*.

Hua was stirring in her sleep. When she was half awake, she made a small chirping noise like a little babbler bird. If I didn't disapper, Hua would disappear. I knew it would be me and I knew it must be soon, before I lost my courage, and before the next morning when the woman would return.

As I sat there in the dark, I made myself feel sad by thinking of what our house would be like without me and wondering whether I would be missed. I was sure my nai nai would not miss me. The only word she ever said to me was *budui*, wrong. She could not forgive me for being a girl.

Ma Ma might miss me, for we sometimes worked shoulder to shoulder in our garden, exclaiming over a rabbit hopping among the peas or a mouse's nest among the cornstalks. I wondered if my ba ba would miss me. When I was small, he would take me by the hand and we would go to see what had sprung out of the earth in the night. He knew one bean tendril from another and one spear of garlic from the other, and they were like so many children to him. Still, when he looked at me, there was always a bit of sadness on his face, as if his eyes had fallen on some misfortune.

Against the leaving behind of my home and my ma ma and ba ba, I set the picture of Hua carried off, crying, her arms stretched out for me. The orphanages were so full of girl babies, there was hardly enough food for the babies to eat. Some of the babies were adopted by *waiguoren*, foreign devils, but some were left hungry and uncared-for in crowded orphanages. There were even stories of selling girl babies to be raised as servants or laborers or worse. I would not let them take Hua. I would be the one to disappear.

three

I waited until everyone was asleep. When all was silent in my parents' room and wheezing whistles came from Nai Nai, I hastily rolled up a change of clothes and took my pencil box, saved from my schooldays. In the days when my parents could afford to send me to school, I had carried the pencil box with me to class each day. I tied the roll with a bit of string. I had a little pile of yuan I was saving in case the day should come when Ba Ba would change his mind about blue jeans. I kissed Hua's cheek lightly. She stirred in her sleep and I held my breath, but she did not awaken. On the courtyard table I placed a note I had written earlier. Only Ba

Ba would be able to read it. I had made it simple, for there were many characters Ba Ba did not know.

Honored Parents,

Now you have only one daughter. A son may yet come.

Your miserable Chu Ju

When I reached the edge of our courtyard, I stopped. In making my plans I had traveled no farther than this. As I stood there, uncertain of where to go, my ye ye's words came back to me. *"There is no end to where the river can take you."*

I hurried along the moonlit path to the deserted village, where the stalls were shuttered like so many closed eyes. I kept to the shadows. A woman disappeared around a corner. A man on a bicycle passed me. Then I was alone. When there are many people about, you are safely hidden in the crowd. Now all the things I feared but could not put a name to were watching me.

At last I came to the river, where a little gathering of fishing boats was tied to the shore. One of the boats had a lantern; the others were dark. Tied to the fishing boats were small boats, each with a heap of netting. At daybreak the boats would pull up their anchors and move up or down the river to a place of good fishing.

I wished I might go with one of the fishermen, but surely he would have nothing to do with the taking of a strange girl onto his boat. I sat at the water's edge listening to the current of the river rocking the fishing boats. The next moment I was creeping softly down the riverbank and climbing into one of the small boats. Little by little I worked my way under the netting. It was no easy task, for the netting was heavy and smelled so strongly of fish, my stomach turned over. I was as tangled in the heavy wet netting as any trapped fish. I would be discovered, but by then perhaps I would be in another place.

As I crouched beneath the netting and the hours passed, I began to see what a foolish thing I had done. I thought of hurrying back, tearing up the note, and climbing into my bed beside Hua. I peeked out and saw along the edge of the dark sky the thin bright line of the coming morning. The next moment I heard a stirring in the fishing boat. A boy with his back to me was peeing over the edge into the water. Hastily I ducked back under the netting. Moments later the boats came alive. There was calling back and forth. I heard the thud of the anchor dropping. Suddenly the fishing boat—with the small boat attached, and me in it—began to move downstream.

I could smell the charcoal burning in a stove and hear a woman calling out that the rice was cooked. I tried to stretch my arms and move my legs a bit, but the netting was too heavy for me. Overhead the sky brightened and a bit of sun found its way to me. A moment later someone stepped on my leg and I cried out.

A boy shrieked, "Ba Ba! A devil is caught in the netting!"

I was afraid they would go after me with one of their sharp fishermen's knives, and I called out, "Please, I am only a girl and mean no harm." The netting was pulled away. I looked up to see a man standing over me. I tried to leap into the water, but the man's hand was around my arm like an iron bracelet. He lifted me from the small boat onto the fishing boat.

"It is only a girl," a woman called out. Two boys, one older than me and the other younger, stood beside the woman staring at me.

The man shook me angrily. "What are you doing on our boat?" he demanded.

While the shaking was going on, I could find no words. The woman said, "Let her be."

The shaking stopped. "I've run away," I said.

"You are a wicked girl," the man scolded. "You must return to your home at once."

I thought he was going to pitch me into the water. "No, please. My ma ma and ba ba are dead, and my nai nai is going to sell me to an evil woman."

The man and the woman looked at me and were silent. Because of Hua, it was a story that had come easily to my head. Though they were for Hua and not me, the tears they saw were real tears, and the fear real fear.

The man said, "We can have nothing to do with such running away. We do not want your misfortune on our boat," but his voice was not so angry.

"Let me stay. I have four yuan for my passage and I can help to clean the fish."

"Four yuan buys nothing," the man said,

"only the rice for a day or two." He looked closely at me. "What do you know of the cleaning of fish?"

"My ye ye was a fisherman." That was nearly the truth. "Until he died I cleaned hundreds of fish for him." That was a lie. Ye Ye had cleaned the few fish he had caught, and I had closed my eyes while he had done it.

"Let the child stay for a bit," the woman said, "until we find out how true her story is."

The two boys only stared at me as if a demon had become tangled in their nets.

The man let go of my arm. "Take care of her, then. Our nets should have been cast long since."

He gave me a push toward the woman. It was only a light push. The anger on his face was gone. He was a strong, stocky man, but I guessed that he would not use that strength unfairly.

With the small boat trailing, we drifted down the river. When man was satisfied, he dropped the anchor. The fishing boat remained moored while the two boys, keeping as far from me as they could, joined their father in the small boat where I had hidden. A moment later they were moving down the river, the man standing at the back of the boat working the oars.

The woman asked, "What is your name, girl?"

I had used up all my lies and only the truth came out.

"Chu Ju," I said.

"Chu Ju," the woman repeated. "Tidy. Let us hope you live up to your name. I am Yi Yi, and my husband is Wu. The older boy is Bo, and the younger Zhong." She bent over the charcoal stove. "Come and have a bit of rice. Then you can help me turn over the fish." She pointed to a bamboo rack where hundreds of small fish were drying. I quickly ate the bowl of rice gruel she handed me and began to turn the fish. It was easily and quickly done.

Yi Yi thrust a bundle of twigs at me. "Give the deck a good scrubbing."

I filled a pail from the river and began the scrubbing. The woman watched me, pointing out here and there where I missed some scales or bits of fish skin that had become stuck to the boat's deck. When I finished, the woman looked pleased.

"We are fortunate in having two sons," she said, "but I would not mind a daughter to keep me company all day on the boat."

Never before had I heard someone talk of her wish for a daughter. "But you already have two children," I said. "You could not have another one."

"No, no," she said quickly. "It is only something I think of from time to time." She gathered up some netting and began to mend a tear.

I watched how clever her fingers were at making knots. "Is that something I could learn?" I asked.

She looked at me for a moment. "Why not? I don't believe you are a stupid girl."

I felt very stupid indeed, for my fingers were so clumsy that I only made the tears larger.

"No, no. Watch me," Yi Yi said. There was no impatience in her voice, only a little amusement.

We worked all morning on the knots, stopping at noon for a bit of rice and fish. My knots were never like Yi Yi's, but in one way or another I mended the tears. Though I had all my worries of leaving Ma Ma and Ba Ba and Hua, and though I did not know at what moment I would be sent from the boat, still, sitting there on the boat was pleasant. A cooling breeze blew down the river and on either bank there was the bright green carpet of new rice shoots. From time to time an excursion boat full of *waiguoren* would pass. They would wave and call out to us in their strange languages, and we would wave back. When another fishing boat would drift by, Yi Yi would hail the fishermen, asking after the success of their catch.

"Wu and our sons are just around the bend," she would call to them. "I hope they will be fortunate. Yesterday's catch was no more than a handful of minnows."

"Ours was not even that," the other fishermen would reply, and I saw that there was no truth telling among the fishermen, for our drying rack and the drying racks of the other fishing boats were crowded with fish.

Yi Yi winked at me. "If we boast of our catch, we will have every fishing boat on the river casting their nets where we cast ours. When we pulled them in, our nets would be empty."

At the end of the day Wu and his sons returned with nets alive with squirming fish. They emptied the nets into the boat. At once everyone went to work. The smaller fish would be cleaned and dried, the larger ones taken whole to the market. I began to grab at the fish as well. Some had their gills caught in the netting and had to be pulled loose in a most cruel way. The fish were slippery in my hands and thrashed about, so for every fish I freed, Bo, who stood beside me, loosened ten. When at last the nets were emptied, the knives came out.

"Here." Wu thrust a wicked-looking knife at me. "You say you have cleaned fish. Get to work."

"Like this," Yi Yi whispered. She picked up an unfortunate fish and slapped it against the deck. The unfortunate fish ceased its flopping and lay silent. With one swipe of her knife the fish was slit open. She reached into the fish's belly and pulled out such a handful of oozing, bloody innards, I had to look away. It was then tossed to Bo and Zhong, who sent a shower of scales over the boat.

I picked up as small a fish as I could find. As I raised it to slap against the deck, its eye fastened onto me. It is a thing with fish that their eyes do not blink, so their stare is pitiful. It was the fish or me. I closed my own eyes and with all my strength slapped the fish against the deck. When I opened my eyes, the fish's eye was still fixed on me and its body moved weakly in my hand. Bo, who was standing beside me, stopped what he was doing and, taking the fish, quickly put an end to it. He tossed it back to me, and I went to work with the knife, sawing a ragged cut rather than the swift clean cut Yi Yi had made. I thrust my hand into that part of the fish I had no wish to know and tugged at the soft mess, tossing it, as the others had, into the river, where a hundred screeching gulls made a meal of it.

Not all the fish's insides ended up in the river. As we worked, the bottom of the boat became slippery with blood and innards. Still we worked on. Hour followed hour until the sun's blaze cooled and the sun was no more than a gold ball slipping into the river. When the last fish was cleaned and pails of water had been thrown on the deck to clean it, I watched in amazement as Wu, Yi Yi, and the boys shed nearly all their clothes and jumped into the river. I stood there, smelly and as covered with scales as any fish. The next moment I was in the river clinging to the boat. The current and gulls had carried the innards away, and the water was nearly clean. The coolness was lovely on my sore hands and back.

Wu and Yi Yi were soon back in the fishing boat, but Bo and Zhong were like otters, slipping here and there, splashing each other and pushing each other under the water. I could not swim, and the river was large and deep. I clung to the boat trembling for fear they would come after me with their splashings and dunkings, but Yi Yi kept an eye on them, and when they came too close to me she warned them, "Mind you leave Chu Ju alone." And they did.

The fish meant for market were loaded into buckets filled with water and the buckets fixed on shoulder poles. Wu and the boys went off with them to the village while Yi Yi and I placed the cleaned fish on the drying racks. When Wu and the boys returned, we ate our evening rice and fish. There was talk of the next place for fishing, and soon the boat was loosed from its moorings and once again we drifted downstream. The fields and villages became hills and then mountains sliced into green steps. As my ye ye had said, there was no end to where the river might carry you. When Ye Ye had spoken, he had been eager for such adventure, but I saw only how far from home the river was taking me.

Yi Yi watched me and saw the sadness on my face. "Tell me about your home," she said, but I only shook my head, for I knew any word I spoke of home would bring enough tears to make my own river.

Wu paid no attention to me. I might have been a small dog underfoot. My lack of skill with the fish had not surprised him, and I was sure he was suspicious of my running away. Had it been up to him, I would have been put ashore long since. It was Yi Yi's pleadings that kept me on the fishing boat, and I believe it was her wish for a daughter that made her plead that I be allowed to stay.

Bo and Zhong did not know what to do with me. Zhong was slim and quick. He darted here and there, happy to startle me with his sudden appearances. In the river he would explode from the water, laughing to see the surprise on my face. I think he did not know what to make of a girl. Bo was more quiet than his brother, going seriously about his work, more a man in what he did than a boy. He frowned at his brother's tricks and was kind to me, though I could see that he, like Zhong, thought me a strange creature.

I became quicker with my knife and less merciful with the fish.

"She earns her rice," Yi Yi said to Wu when he talked again of putting me ashore.

"And if we are questioned as to why there are three children on the boat?" Wu asked.

Yi Yi shrugged. "When have the authorities come onto a poor fishing boat? Each day we are somewhere else. There is no time for suspicion." Still, when we came into a village, Yi Yi set me a task inside the boat's hut.

At first the boys kept their distance, watching as I ate and slept, curious as to how I would do those things. When they saw I ate and slept as they did, they became bolder. Bo taught me the difference between red carp and grass carp. He had many questions about school and what was taught there, for neither Bo nor Zhong had been long enough in a village to go to a school. I brought out my pencil box and drew characters for Bo. I taught him simple ones, such as the character for "earth," which looks like a man standing on the ground, and the character for "claw," which looks just like the claw of a frog. He asked to see the character for "fish." "There is the net," I said, "and there on top is the fish going into it." For that was what the character for "fish" looked like.

Zhong had no questions about school. When Yi Yi was not looking, he put an eel down the back of my shirt and showed me how a frog would still jump with its head cut off.

The worst of the heat and the rain was over, and along the shore the rice plants with their golden kernels had long since been harvested and a winter crop planted. Each day was like the day before, so the months glided on as silently as the boat drifted along the river. The fishing boat was my house, the river was my world. The current rocked me to sleep, and each day there was something new to see—large clumsy barges with their loads of coal, and the many *qing-ting*, the flies with their see-through wings and bright red or green bodies that were narrow as a thread. There were clear days when the sun danced on the water and days when curtains of mist closed over the river and everything disappeared.

The boat became as familiar to me as the home I had left. I knew every inch of it. I could tie a proper knot and coil the ropes neatly. I could mend the nets, leaving no holes for small fish to slip through. I could heartlessly slap a fish against the deck, never minding its staring eye, and the insides of the fish were nothing to me.

Wu said little to me, but he was not unkind.

The boys treated me as they treated each other and teased me, but they were never rough with me. Once Bo and Zhong found a trout tangled in the net. It was a small, slim fish with pink and green and gold coloring on its side. "Like a rainbow," Bo said, and looking to be sure their father did not see, the boys gently put the trout over the side of the boat and watched it swim away. Bo and Zhong treated me as gently as they had treated the trout.

It was Yi Yi who kept me on the boat. Once I heard her call to some woman on a nearby boat, "My husband and the boys are fishing. Only my daughter is with me." How it pleased me to hear the word "daughter." It was because Yi Yi was so kind to me that I made the mistake. Wu and the boys had left for the day, and Yi Yi and I were mending the nets. The winter crop had been harvested, and Yi Yi and I watched a farmer on the shore readying his fields for the planting of the spring rice.

It was the fifth day of the fourth moon, Tomb Sweeping Day. Hua would be celebrating a birthday. Only a year before, Ma Ma and Ba Ba, along with Nai Nai and me, had climbed the path to the tombs of our ancestors. This year they would have Hua with them as they made the journey.

I was sorry that I had deceived Yi Yi, and did not want a lie between us. Without thinking, I confessed that my ma ma and ba ba still lived. I told Yi Yi all about Hua and why I had run away. I was sure she would understand. Instead she was horrified.

"Chu Ju! How could you do such a thing? Think of your poor ma ma. Every minute in her heart she must be worrying about you, wondering where you are. I cannot believe your ma ma would give away her baby. I would never do such a thing."

Quickly I said, "It is different for you. You are

strong. My ma ma is weak. She is afraid of my nai nai. The evil woman had already been to our house. I could not let them take Hua."

But Yi Yi would not listen. "Next week we will be near your village again. You must go home to your parents. I will speak to Wu this evening."

Because of Yi Yi's kind heart and her longing for a daughter, I had thought it was safe to tell my story, but it was that kindness and that longing that made her feel sorry for Ma Ma and made her doubt my story about Hua, for she would never have sent a child of hers away.

In the evening, as the boat floated down the river, Yi Yi whispered my story to an angry Wu. "I will take her myself to her village," he said, and I knew I must escape that night.

I looked about to see what countryside I would find myself in. We had drifted beyond the rice paddies and were in green countryside with many trees. The trees stood in rows, so I knew someone had planted them. Perhaps they were fruit trees of some kind and I could work at picking the fruit. Though Yi Yi might wish to send him, I was sure Wu would not lose a day's fishing by coming after me. He would not know which direction I took, nor would he wish the authorities to ask why a man with two sons was looking for a third child.

It was spring, and the darkness came slowly, yet not too slowly for me, for I did not want to leave the boat that had been my home and where Yi Yi had been like a ma ma and the boys like brothers. Only the night before, when I had exclaimed over fireflies, which I had never seen before, Zhong had waded up a muddy bank to capture some in a glass jar for me. Now I did not know where I could go or what would happen to me.

At last the night came. Overhead there was a new moon shaped like a fingernail paring. In the light of the kerosene lantern that swung from the roof of the boat, I could see everyone was asleep. I had my bundle of clothes, a few dried fish, and the jar of fireflies. I had begun to climb over the edge of the boat when I saw Zhong sit up and stare at me. Had it been Bo, I would have trusted him to be silent, but Zhong always did the first thing that came into his head. To my amazement, what he did now was to keep very quiet. We looked at each other, and then I dropped over the edge and made my way to shore. I was glad I had taken the jar of fireflies. I imagined Zhong following their flickering as I hurried away into the darkness.

four

One place was as dark as another. After many stumbles my feet discovered the smoothness of a path. Following the path until I believed I was far enough from the river, I huddled down to wait for the morning. All about me was the rustle of leaves twitching in the warm breeze. Comforted by the small lights of my fireflies, I fell asleep.

I was shaken awake by a girl no older than myself. Her face was very round and her eyes very large. Her hair stood up in two large tufts tied with string.

"You must be new," she said. "If Ji Rong finds you asleep, he will beat you. Where is your shoulder pole?"

"I have no shoulder pole. Who is Ji Rong?" I saw that the baskets on her shoulder pole were heaped with small green leaves. I looked around at the long rows of trees. "Why are you plucking leaves? Do these trees have no fruit?"

The girl stared at me. "How stupid you are. These are mulberry trees. They are not wanted for their fruit."

At last I understood. Somewhere close by must be the silkworms that fed on the leaves. I gave up my hope of gathering fruit and said, "I need to find work. Will this Ji Rong hire me to gather leaves?"

"You would be a fool to work for him if you did not have to." She rolled up her sleeve to show me ugly black-and-blue marks.

"Why do you stay?"

"I was sent to work here by an orphanage. If I tried to leave, he would come after me and punish me. Anyhow, where would I go? Here I have a bed and food, and at the end of each month a few yuan."

My thoughts flew to Hua. Had I not left, one day she might have been sent from an orphanage to work for someone like this Ji Rong. "I must have work," I said. "Is there no place else?"

The girl gathered up her shoulder pole. She pointed away from the rising sun. "Over there is the place of the silkworms. There is work there, but I would rather have Ji Rong's beatings than the tongue-lashings of the woman." Before I could ask a further question, she hurried away.

I had borne Nai Nai's scoldings, and did not see why I could not bear the scoldings of this woman. I hurried off in the direction the girl had pointed, passing several girls my age and even younger going from tree to tree to gather leaves. If it had not been for their shoulder poles, they could have been playing some game of hide-and-seek among the trees.

I thought the trees would never end, but I came at last to a long, low building. A doorway stood open. From inside the building came a noise such as I had never heard before. I peered inside. Covering long tables were trays of green leaves, and chewing the leaves were thousands of fat white worms. It was their chewing that I had heard. Moving among the tables were women dressed in white smocks, white masks tied around their faces.

A hand reached out and pushed me outside so hard that I fell to the ground. A woman was standing over me. I could not believe so small a woman could give so great a push. Like the girls, she wore a white smock and also a mask, which was tied about the lower half of her wrinkled face. She was old and shriveled, as if all the air had been squeezed out of her. Her gray hair was pulled into a knot on the top of her head, and her narrowed eyes looked at me as Nai Nai had looked upon a cockroach that had crept by night into our rice flour. A moment later the cockroach was dead.

In a whisper she hissed, "You are polluting my worms! How do you dare try to come into this building?"

"Please, I need a job. Could I tend the worms?"

"Never! You would poison my worms with your fishy smell."

"That is only because I lived on a fishing boat. I could clean myself."

Her eyes narrowed even further. "I could not pay you. A bed in the dormitory with the other girls and food. That is all."

A bed and food and safety for a bit. I nodded my head.

"Sit outside, well away from the building," she ordered. "When the girls stop for lunch, I will send one to show you where to go. Scrub yourself and get back here at once. No garlic. My worms don't like it." She caught sight of my jar of fireflies. She snatched it out of my hand and flung it away. With horror I watched it land on a rock and break into pieces.

"What! You would bring dirty bugs near my beauties! There had better be no more stupidities or I will turn you over to the police. Doubtless you have run away after some mischief."

When she left me, I settled down in a bit of shade made by a small stand of bamboo. I did not think the woman would call the police as long as I would work for her without a wage. The sound of the thousands of chewing worms was very loud. All those little mouths at work frightened me. However much I was in want of food and a bed, I did not think I could live each day with such chewing noises. Small as the worms were, they sounded as if they would eat anything in their way.

The sun was overhead when the girls came out

of the building, pulling off their masks and smocks and reaching for pickles and bowls of rice passed to them by a woman who had come loaded with baskets. The day had been hot, and the faces of the girls ran with sweat. One girl hurried over to me, a pigtail bouncing on her back as she ran. In age she was nearly a woman. Her smile was friendly, but she urged me to run alongside her.

"I am Song Su. Quickly. I must get back or Yong will scold me. The worms should be in their fourth hatch today, but they are slow. That always makes Yong cross."

"What do you mean, fourth hatch, and why does that make her cross?"

Song Su opened a door into a long hut built of wood and roofed with metal. It was so hot inside, I could scarcely breathe.

"You'll soon learn," she said. "The worms eat until they are too fat for their skin. They break out of the skin and start eating again. We starve, while the worms get so fat their skin can't hold them. Four times the worms molt, and then they spin the cocoon that makes the silk. This is the dormitory. The shower is in that room. Take any bed that does not have some belongings on the chest that sits next to it. No makeup. The worms don't like the smell." She ran off.

I was happy for the shower's cold water. I scrubbed myself well for the worms and ran back to the building as fast as I could.

"The fish smell is gone," Yong said, "but you could not scrub away the stupid look of a country girl."

She thrust a mask and smock at me. I struggled into the smock and clumsily tied the mask about my face. Yong pulled me over to a table and handed me a feather.

In a whisper she said, "These sweethearts are

yours. They are a little slow in hatching. You must tickle them with the feather like so." She brushed the feather over one of the worms and then another. Seeing her gentleness with the worms, I found it hard to believe she was the same woman who had given me such a push. "Mind you don't miss a single worm or you will not hear the end of it, and no talking. Noise distracts the worms."

I looked quickly around me. There were five other girls with feathers. All afternoon I tickled the fat white worms as they lay on a bed of chopped mulberry leaves chewing away. Baskets of the leaves were brought in to replace the ones that were eaten. Once I thought I saw the girl who had awakened me come with leaves. I tried to catch her eye, but she hurried off.

It was late in the afternoon when one of the girls raised her hand to signal Yong, who ran quickly over to the girl's tray. Another hand was raised.

I saw one of my worms break out of its skin and raised my hand as well. Yong examined the worm and nodded her head. One by one the worms wriggled out of their skins. Once freed, the worms began to wave their heads from side to side, spinning a thin thread and wrapping it about their bodies. I had hated the ugly worms, but now I was fascinated. Here was the silk! By the end of the day all but a few of the worms were spinning their cocoons. The feathers were put away, and we busied ourselves with cleaning the trays, for what went into the worms also came out of them.

It had rained all afternoon, so returning to the dormitory was like swimming through warm water. Little puffs of steam rose from the ground. We hurried through our supper of rice, bean paste, and cabbage, for the dormitory building was so hot no one could bear to stay inside. Outdoors we sat fanning ourselves with leaves from a dying banana tree. Beyond the dormitory and the worm farm, the rows of mulberry trees were silent in the still air. I sat with Song Su and with Jing, the girl who had awakened me. Also with us was Ling Li. As soon as we had come back to the dormitory, Ling Li had put on lipstick and eye shadow. Her jeans were low on her slim hips and allowed her navel to show. What would my ba ba say to that!

The women in the spinning room were older than we were and kept to themselves. I whispered to Jing, who sat beside me, "Look how red those women's hands are."

"They put the cocoons into hot water to loosen the thread, and then they pull the thread," Jing said. "The water is so hot, I don't see how the women stand it, but they say they are used to it."

"Now that the worms are spinning their cocoons, will Yong be less cross?" I asked.

"Oh, no," Song Su said. "This is the worst time

of all, for in three days the cocoons will be spun and all but a few of the worms must die. Yong will be very upset. We hate the spinning of the cocoons."

"Why must the worms die?"

"If they live, they will crawl out of their cocoon, making a hole in it. After that no long thread can be drawn."

Ling Li said, "The killing of the miserable worms is my favorite time. I must live with the worms all day long, and at night I dream of them. They cannot die quickly enough for me. Last week I had to carry baskets of the worms into the town to sell. The owner of the restaurant said, 'Oh, here comes the worm girl.' That is all we are, worm girls."

"But why would you take the worms to a restaurant?" I asked.

"They are a delicacy, fried crisp on the outside and soft as custard on the inside. Yong hates it that we sell her worms. The manager of the silk farm makes her do it because they bring good money."

"Did you come from the same orphanage Jing came from?" I asked Ling Li.

"Yes, most of us did. The orphanage is not far from here, and the manager of the silk farm and the manager of the orphanage have an agreement. As soon as we are sixteen, we are sent to some job. I was sent at fifteen, for the orphanage is so crowded they are anxious to get rid of us."

"Is there no place else for you?" I asked.

"A few of the girls, when they are very young, are taken away by *waiguoren* who come across the ocean to adopt them," Song Su said, "but those are few."

I told them my story of Hua and why I had run away.

Jing sighed. "I only wish someone had run away for me so I could have stayed with my family, but what difference does it make whether it was

Hua or you who ended up here?"

"The orphanage manager put you here," I said. "An orphanage would have put Hua in such a place as well. No one put me here. I came by myself and I can go."

"Where can you go?" Song Su asked. "It's dangerous for a girl traveling alone. Only last month we heard how a girl who ran away was kidnaped. Girls are sold to men who are in need of wives. So many girl babies have been lost, there are more men than women."

I could not say where I would go, for I had no idea. I only knew that I would not be a worm girl all my life.

What Song Su had said was true. The next morning Yong was in a terrible temper. Once the worms had spun their cocoons, the cocoons were carried away to a room where they were heated so the worms inside them died. Only a few worms were allowed to hatch and lay eggs so there would be more worms. Yong watched as the trays of cocoons were carried off.

"Ah, my beauties," she moaned.

She ordered us to scrub the floors and the tables so that they would be ready for the next shipment of worms. No matter how hard we scrubbed, we could not please her.

There were no worms now, so Yong had no need to hiss and whisper her words. "Song Su," she shrieked. "You have left your dirty footprints on the freshly scrubbed floor. Do it over. Chu Ju, none of your filthy country ways. The undersides of the tables must be as clean as the tops."

The windows and walls were scrubbed as well, for there was always the chance that some worm disease would infect the new worms and they would perish.

Ling Li whispered, "I wish I knew of such a

disease. I would spread it everywhere."

When at last the new worms arrived, Yong seemed almost cheerful. "Ah, look at the poor babies. They need fattening. Come, move quickly," she ordered us, "see that the leaves are thickly spread." Once more we heard the chewing.

My days were chewed away as well in the long hours of caring for the worms. Ling Li, Song Su, Jing, and I became friends. After our workday was over, we would sit outside for the breezes. Chewing on sunflower seeds or sucking on pieces of sugar-cane for the sweetness, we would tell one another our worries and hopes.

When Yong shouted and scolded one of us, we could be sure the others would sympathize, making faces behind Yong's back. We called Yong Mouth of a Thousand Serpents. We also had a name for Ji Rong: Biting Dog. Ling Li let us try her makeup and Song Su let me try on her jeans. There was no talk of families, for the orphanage girls had no memories of a ma ma or ba ba. I never mentioned my own family, for I did not want to speak of what they did not have, but often I thought of my own ma ma and ba ba and of Hua. She would be taking her first steps. I wondered if I would still recognize her. The dormitory sheltered me, but it was not the home I dreamed of.

Though Yong still scolded me each day, after a few months she saw that I was given a few yuan when the other girls received theirs. "You are as worthless as they are, so why should you not have what they have," she said. After that I did not mind her scoldings as much.

In February we celebrated the New Year, the year of the Golden Dragon. Night after night fireworks were set off, the sky exploding into fiery flowers of color. Day after day we heard the sound of the drums that accompanied the lion dances.

People in their red clothes crowded into the shops to buy mandarin cakes and dumplings with little coins hidden inside. Yong, reminding us that in preparation for the New Year it is traditional to sweep and scrub, set us to cleaning the dormitory, then scolded us for making a poor job of it. Yet on the night when families gathered for the custom of eating a whole fish together, Yong remembered we were orphans, and instead of our usual cabbage and rice, she provided us with a huge carp in a fragrant sauce. We spent money on lanterns, which we hung in the dormitory. As we tied on red ribbons and scarves and sat down to our feast as a family, I couldn't help thinking of Ma Ma and Ba Ba and wondering if they were celebrating the New Year. I wondered if they thought of me and if I had a brother.

All my problems came about from a good deed. It was the fourth moon, and I had been with the worms for nearly a year. Though it was not the time of the rains, one afternoon a great storm came. There was lightning and thunder. Yong paced up and down the aisles peering into the trays, crooning to the worms, "Don't worry, my little ones. It is only a small storm, and it will pass away."

The door opened and I saw Jing hurry in. I thought she had come with leaves for the worms, but her baskets were nearly empty. She crouched in one corner of the room, a frightened look on her face. Before Yong could say anything, the door opened and Biting Dog burst into the room, grabbed Jing, and pulled her outside into the storm.

At dinnertime Jing sat by herself with her head down. She would not look at us. In the evening I heard her crying softly in the cot next to mine. When I asked what was wrong, she only shook her head and cried harder. I sat beside her and waited. Finally the crying stopped and Jing sat up. On her cheek was an evil-looking black-and-blue mark.

"When the lightning and thunder came," she said, "I was afraid to be under so many trees, but Biting Dog said the worms must eat and the leaves must be collected. I ran away, and he came after me and beat me with a stick."

"Jing, do you think the orphanage knows that Biting Dog beats the girls?"

She shook her head. "No. When the people from the orphanage come to inspect the worm farm, everyone here is very nice to us. That is all the orphanage sees."

"The next time they come, you should tell the orphanage people the truth."

"We are never allowed to talk with anyone from the orphanage. We are watched every min-ute."

"Then you must write a letter to the orphan-age," I said.

"How am I to do that?" Jing looked sadder

than ever. "We were never taught to write at the orphanage. They said we would be workers and would have no need."

"I'll write the letter for you," I promised. "Yong and Biting Dog will never know who sent it." But when I said that, I stupidly forgot that it would be no secret to them that no one from the orphanage could write.

The writing of the letter was a great thing. Only the four of us knew of it, and together we made our plans. After dinner we hurried along the Path of the Squawking Crows to the nearby village. The village was a small affair of dirt streets and stalls. There was a teahouse where old men sat playing checkers. Many of the men had brought their birdcages, and the birds fluttered about beating their wings against the wire caging. A melon peddler cried his wares, and there was a noodle shop and a stall where bicycles were repaired. We headed for the small store where Ling Li got her makeup. After much consultation we bought paper, an envelope, and a stamp.

That night we huddled together in a corner of the dormitory. The girls watched as I brought out my pencil and notebook. I waited to hear what I should say.

"Tell them about the poor food," Ling Li said.

"Tell them about the heat of the dormitory," Song Su said.

"And the beatings," from Jing.

When the letter was written, it was passed from hand to hand and held for a few minutes as if each of the girls wished to have some part in the writing of the letter. They made me read it to them again and again.

Honored Orphanage Manager:

   All is not well here at the silk farm. We have no meat or fish to eat, only rice and cabbage and sometimes bean paste and pickles. The dormitory

has no breeze that comes into it, only heat. Worst
of all, Yong scolds us all day and Ji Rong beats us.
Please come and let us show you the black-and-blue
marks.

The Orphans

The letter was sealed carefully in an envelope, each one of us licking a bit of the flap. The next evening we returned to the town, and after looking all about to be sure no one from the silk farm was watching, we mailed the letter.

All week we waited, hardly daring to look at one another. With each angry look from Yong we were sure she had discovered what we had done. At the end of the week an orphanage worker came. She was as big as a man, so she towered over Yong and even Biting Dog, but her voice was kind. When she looked at us, she did not smile with her mouth but she smiled with her eyes, and none of us were afraid of her. Though Yong and Biting Dog complained loudly and said the girls were sure to be untruthful, one by one the woman called all the girls from the orphanage to talk with her. Yong and Biting Dog were not allowed to hear what was said. After the orphanage worker left, Ling Li whispered, "I told her of the bugs in the cabbage."

"She saw for herself how hot the dormitory was," Song Su said.

"I showed her my black-and-blue marks," Ying said, "and she was very angry."

After that the food was better, a fan was put in the dormitory, and Biting Dog only growled and no longer struck the girls. Yong was furious that such a letter had been sent, but she could not find out from the orphanage who sent it and she did not dare to punish all of us for fear there would be another visit from the orphanage worker. If the orphange sent their girls somewhere else, the silk farm would be in trouble, for where could they get such cheap labor?

Still, Yong knew the orphans could not write and she watched me closely. One day she came to me and, with a crafty look, said, "I don't have enough time to keep track of the number of worms we get. Here is a notebook. You can put down the day the worms come and the numbers of worms. If you are careful with the records, I might pay you a larger wage."

I shook my head. "I cannot write, Yong," I said. "I am only a stupid country girl."

She gave me a suspicious look but said nothing more. That night I found my pencil box had been stolen from my chest. I truly hated Yong and longed to go to her and demand that she return it, but I had told her I could not write.

The next day as soon as I entered the worm room, Yong said to me, "We have more girls than we need. You must leave at once. You can go back to the country. Doubtless you can find a job cleaning out pigpens. It is all you are suitable for."

Song Su and Ling Li were watching. I longed to bid them *zai-jian*, but Yong forbade me to speak to anyone. As I reached the door, Song Su and Ling Li ran to me and put their arms around me until Yong hissed to them to return to the worms.

When I went to the dormitory to get my bundle of clothes, I was amazed to find the pencil box. Yong had returned it. I thought I had seen into Yong as far as a person could go, but I had not. There was yet a bit of heart in her, so when I left, I was not quite so afraid for my friends.

five

I don't know how long I would have stayed among the worms. Though I had boasted that I might go where I wished, I knew of no place to go. I longed to return to the river and to Ma Ma and Ba Ba and Hua, but I made myself turn away from the direction of the river and my home.

Except to buy a bit of food, I kept away from villages, for the stories Jing had told about young girls being kidnaped frightened me. At night I slept curled up in a bamboo grove. As one day followed another, the whole countryside changed before my eyes. The rows of mulberry trees were gone. All around me were small and large rice paddies, the flooded paddies marked off by mud dams no more than a foot high. The paddies were dotted with the wide circles of bamboo hats as the farmers bent over to plant the new rice shoots.

The paths that wound through the paddies were muddy, sucking at my feet. I had no bamboo hat, so as the day grew hotter, the sun became scorching. The mosquitoes buzzed around my head. I longed to be back with the worms, where there was a roof over my head, food at the end of the day, and friends to talk with.

I stopped at each paddy to ask if a worker was needed. The farmer would look at me, and seeing I was only a young girl, he would shake his head. I had left the large paddies where there were many workers and had come to small rice fields separated by dams that held the few inches of water needed to grow the rice. Beyond the paddies was higher ground where fields of sugarcane and jute grew.

At one of the smallest paddies a woman and a man worked at tucking the young rice seedlings into the mud that lay beneath the water. The woman moved slowly, and from time to time she stood up to rest her back. She was dark from the sun, thin as one of the rice shoots, and though she looked to be no more than fifty, she was stooped from years of planting. I saw that she was watching the young man, a worried look on her face. The man went about his work as if he were furious with the rice seedlings, plunging them into the water as if he were drowning them instead of planting them.

Though it was only a small paddy and unlikely to need another worker, the woman looked so tired, I gathered my courage once more and asked of her, "Is it possible that you could use a worker here?"

The man took no notice of me, but the woman looked up from her planting, a puzzled expression

on her face, as if she were searching for this worker
I was talking of.

"I'm not afraid of work. I tended crops in a
large plot."

The woman smiled. "We could use the help,
for even this small place is too much for me and my
son, but we have no money for another worker,
even for one so young as you."

No grown person had smiled at me in a long
time, and while the short, angry refusals of the
other farmers had not hurt me, by now I was tired
and miserable and the little kindness was too much
for me. I burst into tears and began to run away.

"Wait!" the woman called after me. I stopped
and looked back. The man and woman were argu-
ing with each other. The woman waved me back.

"*Chi fan meiyou?*" she asked.

"Have you eaten yet?" is a common greeting,
but I saw that she meant for me to tell the truth. I

shook my head, for the food I had bought with the few yuan I had saved had long since been eaten.

"We have no money, but we have rice," she said. "Rest a bit while we finish, and you can share our dinner." The young man had gone back to his planting, punishing the rice shoots more fiercely than ever.

For an answer I took up a basket of shoots and asked how they were planted. The woman smiled again, and taking my hand, she guided it to the mud beneath the water and made a hole in the mud. "Like this," she said, and placed two shoots in the hole, firming the mud about the tender roots. "You must be sure to see that the mud hugs the roots, or a wind will come along and the shoot will float loose."

After the woman was satisfied with my work, she attended to her planting, but I caught the man looking at me from time to time as if he were considering me in a way I did not understand.

When the last of the shoots were planted, the woman and the young man stood in the path examining their arms and legs, pulling at something that clung to them. With horror I saw they were pulling off fat, black leeches. I looked at my own arms and legs, and discovering three of the ugly worms clinging to my skin, I began to scream. The woman hurried over and showed me how to sprinkle onto the leeches a bit of salt, which she carried in a bag around her neck. Salted, the leeches curled up and dropped away.

"After you have done it a thousand times," she said, "you will think nothing of it."

I had believed I was finished with worms. At least, I thought, the silkworms were satisfied with mulberry leaves and did not cling to you as if they wished to suck away your very lifeblood. Together we walked toward a wooden house. In the back of the house was a square of garden. The house was much like my own home had been, with two small rooms and a tiny courtyard. Everything was tidy. The bamboo mats on the floor had been swept. The two windows sparkled. Neatly braided strings of garlic and onions hung on the wall. On a small shelf was a picture of an old man.

Han Na, for I had learned that was the woman's name, set a fire and put the rice on to boil while her son, Quan, brought water from a nearby well so that we could all rid ourselves of the mud from the paddy. While we stood in the courtyard, splashing ourselves, Han Na asked my name and where I had come from.

"Chu Ju," I said. "I come from an orphanage." It was a small lie, but when I had told my true story to Yi Yi on the fishing boat, she had wanted to take me back to my home. I would not make the same mistake. I could see that Quan resented every grain of rice I ate, and I was sure I would be sent on my way in the morning, but for now this good woman and her small nest were so pleasant to me, I didn't wish to risk having to leave at once.

Han Na asked no more questions, but as we sat at our rice in the courtyard, she said, "It is a sad thing that so many of our country's children should be scattered about like leaves." She looked at her son, who threw down his chopsticks.

"Of course they are scattered," he said in a cross voice. "How are farmers to make a living when their land measures no more than five *mu*? After we pay our lease fees and taxes, there is hardly enough for the next year's seed. How can a man live unless he leaves the land and finds work in the city? There you can make three times as much as you make on the land."

Han Na said, "In the city you are one among millions, everything is unknown, and nothing is yours. Here every inch of the land is familiar. I could close my eyes and find my way anywhere on our land. Can you say the same for a city like Shanghai?"

Quan seemed taken aback by her words, but he answered, "Why should you not learn to know a city as well as the mud of a paddy?"

When the bowls were washed, though my back ached and my feet were sore, with no word I went out into the little garden beside the house and began to weed among the yam vines and the cabbage, pulling out the thistles and grasses that choked the vegetables and shooing the chickens that clucked around me. When I came in, I picked up my things, ready to leave.

"Wait," Quan said. "If you wish, you can stay a few days. We can use help with the planting of the rice. There will be food and a bed."

At the time I was surprised that the invitation came from Quan and that Han Na added no words of welcome. It was only at the end of the week that

I understood why Quan wanted me to remain and why Han Na, kind as she was, worried at my staying, for Quan announced that he was leaving for Shanghai.

"You have no government permit to go to the city," Han Na said. "What will you do when there is a *cha hukou*, a checking of residence permits? You will be arrested."

"How can the police check everyone in a city of many millions?" Quan looked at me. "You have the girl now. She can plant and weed as well as I do. I will send you money each month, and one day you can leave this backbreaking labor and live an easier life." His voice grew soft and pleading. "Ma Ma, it isn't just that I have no wish to spend the rest of my days in the mud of the paddy, it is that I cannot bear to see you bent over from morning to night. If you go on like this, you will die working in the paddy as Ba Ba died."

I had listened to only a part of what Quan said.

I had not gotten beyond the words, "You have the girl now." Were there to be days in Han Na's house beyond this one? I put my hands in my lap so their trembling would not be seen.

"We have seen your pencil box," Quan said. "Is it possible you read and write?"

"I am not greatly skilled."

Quan asked, "You could read any letters I send?"

I nodded. "If they were simple."

"I could write only simple letters."

Han Na said, "It may be that your coming is a fortunate thing, seeing as how Quan is determined to go." She sighed. "Or your coming may have brought closer the misfortune of Quan's going. I cannot tell. I have very little, but what I have I will share with you for as long as you wish to stay."

I hid my face in my hands. "As long as you will have me," I mumbled.

There is a cuckoo that hides in the daytime but

at night you sometimes hear his call. That night I heard the cuckoo calling and I took it for a good omen. I slept soundly. When I awoke in the morning to the crowing of the rooster, I was still in the house of Han Na but Quan had left.

six

Han Na went about with red eyes and so sad a face, I could not bear to look at her. Several times she went to the door and peered out as if Quan might return, but there was no returning of Quan. She rolled up Quan's mattress and put it away, but she left his bowl on the table and there it stayed, a small bit of him, day after day.

In spite of her sadness she let none of her tears fall onto the rice seedlings. Han Na was up early in the morning, and by daybreak we were in the paddy attacking the weeds that grew faster than the rice and, had we not pulled them out, would have choked the rice to its death. Early in the mornings a mist hung over the paddy, so wading into the paddy was like wading into the clouds. Then the sun punished us. The only shade was the two moving circles made by our hats.

It was the time of the rains, and every afternoon a warm rain would fall, making little dimples on the water. When the rice grew to cover the water, the rain fell on the rice plants and they sprang up into a thick green mat.

Han Na was sad, but it was not all sadness. A little frog would jump out at us and I would see a smile come over Han Na's face. The frog would go into her bag and its tender flesh would make our rice tasty that night.

Often Han Na would tell me to rest. "You are not used to such work. If Quan is not going to work the land when I am gone, what is the use of breaking our backs to save it?" Still, Han Na worked on. I saw that it did not matter how the land tired her out. It was her land, and every *mu* was precious to her.

The work was hard but I was not unhappy. Han Na was kind, sharing with me all that she had. After our evening rice we would sit in the court-yard, where there was a breath of air, and look out at the green patchwork of rice paddies and beyond the paddies at the hills where the clouds gathered. Often Han Na would tell me stories of the land.

"My family has always worked this land," Han Na said, "but long ago all the land belonged to a very rich man and they worked for him."

Han Na's grandmother had told her of the great house in which the rich man lived. "The women were dressed in the finest silks, and around their necks hung jade and pearls," Han Na said. "Their feet were cruelly turned back on themselves and bound until they were no larger than a child's hand. They could only totter about and had to be carried everywhere. The landlord kept strange animals, monkeys and tigers. He had more wives than he could remember. The Revolution took the land from him, but not before putting him and his whole family to death. We have some of his land now," Han Na said, "but we must wade in his blood to grow our rice."

Even more wonderous to me than Han Na's tales was the rice itself. Though my back never ceased to ache, I thought how happy Ba Ba would be to see the rice plants spring up, green and tall in the paddies.

While I marveled at the rice growing before my eyes, Han Na grew weaker and lived only for Quan's letters. It was a month before the first letter arrived.

Honored Ma Ma,

I am now in the great city of Shanghai. It is larger than can be imagined. There are more people

in this city than there are grains of rice in our whole
province. The food and the language are strange, so
you cannot be sure you are still in China. People get
from one part of the city to the other by descending
underground and riding cars through tunnels that
have been burrowed into the ground. As yet there is
no job for me, but new buildings rise everywhere, so
labor must be wanted. Tell me how the rice is
progressing. I send my greetings to the girl.

> *Your humble son,*
> *Quan*

Han Na had me read Quan's letter several
times, trying to find comfort in his words, but there
was little comfort in the story of a son lost in a large
city with no friends and no work and perhaps no
roof over his head or food to eat.

Another month went by, and Quan's next letter
told of work and a room he shared with several

other laborers. In the letter after that there were yuan notes wrapped in paper. "Buy a little meat to keep up your strength," Quan wrote to his mother, "and a new quilt to take the place of the worn one." But Han Na carefully put the yuan, still wrapped in its paper, into the chest where she kept her few clothes.

Once a week Han Na sent me into the village for salt or noodles or on some other small errand. The journey was pleasant, for the path into the village wandered among the rice paddies and I rejoiced in standing upright all day. I would stop here and there to compare the crops of the other paddies with our crop. I worried if another crop was further along than ours, and I was pleased if our crop was taller and thicker. I would exchange a word with the other farmers and learn from them. One farmer showed me a new way of planting the rice seedlings. "You throw the seedlings," he said.

"Won't they float away?" I asked.

"No. The weight of the small clump of dirt that clings to their roots will settle them into the earth. It is much faster."

In the village the streets were crowded with bicycles. You had to step carefully, for the people of the village threw their refuse out of their doorways onto the walks, and there was much spitting. Also there was the smell of nightsoil coming from the privies behind the houses and shops. The holes beneath the privies were shallow so that the men who collected the nightsoil for crops would have no difficulty. Train tracks ran through the village, and if I was lucky, I might see one of the great beasts as it came to a screeching halt to unload or pick up passengers. Many of the trains rushed along without stopping, for our village was not an important one.

If I went early in the morning, I would be

in time to see the villagers at their martial-arts exercises. Drums and gongs were sounded and the villagers practiced making war with clubs, swords, pitchforks, and even umbrellas.

I lingered among the shops. In one shop there were cages of quacking ducks. In another ribbons of live eels squirmed among the fish, and for a moment I was sad thinking of Wu and the boys and Yi Yi. There was a stall where keys were made and another where you could find bamboo hats in every size and shape. A doctor had set up a booth, and hanging on the wall of his booth was an acupuncture chart exactly like my ba ba's. My favorite place was the Morning Sun Noodle Shop, where noodles, longer than I was tall, were cut from endless rolls of dough. Han Na always gave me a few yuan for a bowl of the noodles nestled in a bit of fragrant broth. I sipped the long worms of noodles slowly, making them last, and then I would stand a bit by the teahouse to look at the old men and their caged birds. I was fascinated to see how from a great distance the clever waiter directed the stream of boiling water into the cups. When I hurried home, I would tell Han Na all that I had seen in the village.

I tried to get her to go with me, but she would not leave the land. Though months had passed since Quan had left, I believe she still expected him to return, for often she would stand at the door, her hand shading her eyes looking into the distance.

One evening a man came walking toward us, and Han Na let out an exclamation and took a step toward him. Then she stopped. "It is only Ling."

"Who is Ling?" I asked.

"The Zhangs live in the hills. Ling's ba ba was a friend of my husband's. Each week they played checkers together at the teahouse in the village. It is the Zhangs' water buffalo who plows our paddy each spring. Ling is a good boy, but he is a boy who will do what he wants. His ba ba raises wheat, but Ling goes his own way."

As Ling came closer, I saw that he was young, perhaps not yet twenty. He was as long and thin as a noodle. A wing of black hair fell over his eyes. He wore glasses, but behind the glasses his eyes were bright and questioning. He bowed to Han Na and looked at me with surprise.

"Ba Ba said there was talk in the village that Quan had left to work in the city," he said. "My parents wondered how you managed the paddy on your own." All the while he spoke, he looked at me as if he were trying to find a reason for my being there.

"What they say is true. He left in the middle of the fourth moon. We have letters from him." In a proud voice Han Na added, "And money." Seeing that Ling was still staring at me, she said, "This is Chu Ju. She came as Quan left. She takes his place in the paddy." Han Na gave me a sad smile. "She is my son now."

Ling grinned at me in a friendly way, showing no surprise that I should appear to take Quan's place. He thrust a basket at Han Na. "Ba Ba sent this."

The basket held a heavy bag of flour for noodles and five perfect peaches.

In a proud voice Ling said, "The peaches are mine."

"Your young trees have fruit already!"

"Yes, and plums are there as well." His smile nearly filled his whole face. "Next year I will have fruit to take into the village to sell."

"Will you drink tea with us?" Han Na asked.

Ling shook his head. "Thank you—I must return." He looked in the direction of the paddy. "You have no fish in your paddy yet?"

"Fish in the rice paddy." Han Na laughed. "What nonsense is that?"

Ling's smile was gone and he looked very earnest. "No, it is not nonsense. I told Quan. When I was getting my own pamphlet on raising fruit, I saw one on raising fish. It said the agricultural agent will give you fingerlings, and the tiny fish will grow into carp. The carp will eat the weeds. Then you can harvest the fish as well as the rice." He spoke as if he were reading from a pamphlet.

Han Na shook her head. "Those fish swim in your pamphlet. In the paddy they would never swim."

I liked the idea of the little fish swimming among us in the paddy, eating the weeds. "Where can you get the tiny fish for the paddy?" I asked.

Ling, who had looked unhappy at Han Na's scorn, now smiled again. "In the village there is a government office. They got me my little trees, and they could get you the tiny fish, but it must be done in the early spring before the rice shoots are planted."

Ling bowed to us and hurried away toward the hills.

"He is a good boy," Han Na said, "but from the time he was a little boy, he had his nose in one of his pamphlets. What good can come from that?"

I looked at the five perfect peaches and thought if he had found the way to make such peaches in a pamphlet, that was surely good.

The rice had flowered, and now the grains fattened and turned to gold. "In another week we will harvest," Han Na said, but before we could harvest the grains, the starlings came. As we walked to the paddy, we saw the sky was dark with the birds. Their hoarse shrieks pierced my ears and rattled my brain. Han Na ran at them, striking left and right with her hoe. "They will destroy us," she wailed.

"We must have a scarecrow," I said, remembering the scarecrow that was so frightening to me in our garden at home.

We took some old clothes Quan had left behind and stuffed them with paddy straw. On the scarecrow's head we put Han Na's old bamboo hat. At the sight of the scarecrow most of the starlings few off, but a few perched on the scarecrow, so Han Na and I took turns staying in the paddy in the early evenings when the birds fed.

As I sat alone at the edge of the paddy ready to strike out with my hoe, the scarecrow reminded me so of my home that it was all I could do not to make my way down the path and begin the journey that would take me back. It was hard to remember now what Hua looked like and how she had felt in my arms. She would be three years old and walking. I tried to imagine what Ma Ma and Ba Ba would say if I returned. I knew I could be sure of Nai Nai's scolding. Han Na was kind to me, and hard as the work was, I was happy helping to make the rice grow. But Han Na was not my ma ma and her house was not my home. I grew sad, and then the starlings came and I ran about threatening them with my hoe and after a while I forgot my sadness.

At the end of the eighth moon we harvested the rice with our scythes and beat the rice on the threshing stone to rid it of its hull and the bran. The pure white kernels that emerged were like so many pearls. Nothing was wasted. The sweet-smelling straw was saved to stuff our mattresses and to make nests for the chickens. The bran that covered the white kernels was given to the Zhangs to feed the water buffalo who would plow our land for the next crop of rice. We measured out enough rice to feed us. In the measuring Han Na counted Quan, even though he was not there.

"We will have it if he returns," she said.

The rest of the crop was sold to a man who called at all the paddies, haggling over the price and paying too little. Still, Han Na was able to add to the savings that now came every month from Quan and rested in the chest. She often took out the money and counted it to see how it grew. "One day," she said, "there will be enough for Quan to come home."

When the rice was sold, Han Na handed me some yuan. "Certainly your work should be rewarded," she said.

"What am I to do with it?" I asked.

"As you like," she said.

I went to the village and stood by the stall that sold blue jeans. Finally I got up my courage and, asking the price, found I had enough yuan to buy a pair.

"What size?" the woman asked.

I knew nothing of size since my ma ma and nai nai had made my clothes. They were always large for me, so that I would not grow out of them too quickly, and then after a while they were too small.

"Try these," the woman said. I went behind a curtain and pulled them on. When I saw they fit, I folded up my trousers and, keeping on the jeans, put the money in the woman's hand. There was still a little money, and I bought Han Na candied ginger, which was her favorite thing to eat, and her smile was nearly as pleasant to me as the blue jeans.

seven

It was time to plant the winter crop—radishes, cabbage, sweet potatoes, melons, and squash. When spring came, the paddy would be flooded and the rice planted again. As we worked in the field, it saddened me to see how easily Han Na tired. If she stood up suddenly, she became dizzy and I would have to steady her. Though I begged her to leave the work to me, she would not return to the house and would only rest for a bit in the shade of the bamboo.

The rains had long since ended and the weather was pleasant. I often looked at the hills and wondered how Ling's orchard was doing, for it was cooler there, and then one day Han Na said, "It is time to visit the Zhangs." Han Na was not one to accept charity. Though the Zhangs' gift of wheat flour was kindly meant, the gift weighed on her. "I must take them something in return," she said. After that she fell upon our fattest chicken and imprisoned it in a basket.

I washed my hair, leaving it fall to my shoulders with no ponytail.

Han Na looked at me with surprise. "Now you are more a young woman than a girl," she said. She was in her best jacket and trousers, and I wore my new blue jeans. Together we set off with the restless chicken. It grew cooler as we went up the hill, climbing slowly so as not to tire Han Na. The winter wheat on the farms we passed trembled in the light winds. The bamboo groves swayed and rustled. Many of the farms on the hill had pigs, and one or two, like the Zhangs', had a water buffalo.

The houses were as large as three rooms. Everywhere there was stone that had been cleared from the land. The houses were made of stone, the fences were of stone, and wherever you looked there were piles of stone waiting to be put to some use.

The Zhangs must have been prosperous, for they lived in one of the three-room houses. Ling and his parents hurried to greet us, apologizing for the climb up the hill and for the disorder of the house, which in truth was as neat as Han Na's house.

They made much of Han Na's gift of a chicken. We were given bowls of tea to drink and pickled ginger and dumplings in broth. It was a mystery where Ling's height came from, for his parents were like two dolls, small and very neat in appearance.

While the Zhangs talked with Han Na about Quan, Ling offered to show me his orchard. On the way we passed the stable where the Zhangs' water buffalo was tethered. I stopped to stare at the great animal. "Is he dangerous?" I asked, looking at the beast's curved horns.

"He is a great baby," Ling said. He reached over and patted the beast, who rolled his eyes at us. "I have ridden him since I was five years old and had to be tied onto his back to keep from falling off. In the spring the buffalo and I will be down to plow Han Na's rice paddy and all the nearby paddies. When I come, I'll give you a ride on the buffalo if you like."

Ling's orchard clung to the hillside with only a high stone wall like two sheltering arms to keep the trees safe. There were twenty trees, some full-grown and some Ling's height and a few no taller than I.

"Each year I clear more stones and bring in more dirt," Ling said. "Where there was nothing, there is land now." One by one he introduced me to his trees, which in the winter season had lost their leaves. "This plum has a golden color like the wheat when it ripens, and this one is lavender like the twilight sky in the eleventh moon." He stood frowning at a tree. "These peaches are sweet but very small. When I take them to market, no one buys them. They look at the size and won't believe in the sweetness."

After I had met each tree, we sat at the edge of the orchard and Ling told me of the trees that were to come when more stones were moved and more dirt brought in. "I do not understand how Quan could have left the land for the city," he said. "In the city when you sit down to rest at the end of the day, there are no stretches of green paddies or rising hills to see, only ugly buildings and dirty streets."

"Ling," I asked, "how did you know how to plant and care for such trees?"

The great smile took over his face. "There are pamphlets in the village, which the government gives out for the asking. I have a box full of pamphlets. You can find your fish in one of their pamphlets. I could show you the place in the village." In a low voice he said, "It is one good thing among many bad things the government does." Then he asked, "Can you read?"

I nodded my head.

That seemed to please Ling. "I have as many books as trees. Some of them are foreign stories. I could lend you one."

He took me back to the buffalo stable. There was a shelf of books. "Why do you keep your books here?" I asked. "The beast does not read."

Ling shrugged. "It's closer to the orchard. Sometimes I stop my work and read for a bit." He added, again in the quiet voice, "Though they can't read, it is best that my parents do not see my books. My parents would think some of the words in the books dangerous."

"Dangerous?"

"Dangerous only because they speak the truth."

Each book was wrapped carefully in a piece of newspaper.

"It keeps them safe from bugs and dampness," Ling said, but I thought he had not said all he wished.

"But how do you know which book is which?" I asked.

"From their shapes," Ling said, "and where they are on the shelf. Here is one for you to read, *A Dream of Red Mansions*. It was written more than two hundred years ago." He handed me a heavy book.

"So long ago?" I asked. "Why read it now?"

The smile came again. "Do you think people change? Anyhow, it's China's greatest book."

I nodded my head.

That seemed to please Ling. "In our house I

have a pamphlet on squash and still another on radishes, all of which I know Han Na plants. I'll lend them to you."

When we returned to the Zhangs' house, Ling filled my hands with pamphlets, handling them as if they might be precious jewels.

His father laughed. "Ling farms with his pieces of paper as well as his hoe, but as long as his trees do well, I will say nothing against the pieces of paper."

As Han Na and I made the return trip down the hill, Han Na said, "Ling seemed pleased with you." After a moment she added, "Chu Ju, I have never asked you about your parents or the orphanage that you say you come from. I have only been glad to have you, but others, such as Ling's parents, might be curious. They might wonder if you have anything to hide."

"I have nothing to hide," I said. "My parents

are honorable people. My father, though only trained for a short time, is a doctor."

"I will ask you no more of your family," Han Na said, "but it may be that one day you will want to visit them."

For an answer I only shook my head, but sooner than I imagined I was indeed telling Han Na of such a visit. It was a terrible lie, and it came about in this way. I returned from the village with a letter to Han Na from Quan. As usual she opened it and handed it to me to read. For the first time in many months the letter contained no yuan, but Han Na said nothing of that. It was always Quan's words she looked for and not the money. The first part of the letter was short and much as usual. Beneath the usual part were these frightening words.

This is for the girl's eyes only. *I am in jail. There was a* cha hukou. *The police searched our room and caught all who had no residence permits. Unless a fine is paid for me, I must remain in the detention center. Take the train and come to this address with all the money I have sent. You must not mail it or the jailers will steal it. Do not tell Ma Ma, for it would kill her. Quan*

The letter shook in my hand.

"What is it?" Han Na asked.

"I feel a little sick," I said. "The broth in my bowl of noodles tasted strange."

"Ah," Han Na said, "they are sloppy at the noodle shop. Who knows what was in your bowl? Drink a little boiled water and lie down for a bit and rest."

I drank the boiled water and said, "I think the air would make me better." Gratefully I escaped, and as soon as I was out of sight of the house, I sank down in a bamboo grove. I had read Quan's words only once, but I knew them by heart as surely as if they were cut into my brain with a knife. Everything he asked was impossible. I must steal the money from Han Na. I must find a way to get onto the train. It must be a train that would take me to Shanghai. In Shanghai, a city of millions, with who knew how many thousands of streets and turnings, I must go to the detention center and find Quan. Each thing was more impossible than the other. My heart sank within me. I would tell Han Na, and we would go together. But Han Na tired easily these days, and to learn that Quan had been arrested might truly kill her.

All the rest of the day and all the night I turned over Quan's dreadful words. The next day when our work was done, I said to Han Na, "This book that Ling gave me to read is too difficult. May I take it to him and ask for another?"

Han Na laughed. "You were never a girl to find something too difficult, but if you wish to see

Ling again, one excuse is as good as another."

I blushed at what she was suggesting, but I had to have someone's help and there was only Ling. It might be that he had a train pamphlet or even a Shanghai pamphlet. I believed the boy who made an orchard from stones would understand how a thing must be done.

I hurried past the Zhangs' home hoping I would not be seen and made my way to the orchard. Ling was standing at the edge of the orchard, his arm stretched out, and perched on his hand was a hawk. The hawk flew off and I watched it soaring over the paddies and fields. For a moment I forgot my trouble, amazed that Ling should have held a wild bird in his hand. I called softly to Ling and he looked around, startled at my voice. Then a great smile came over his face.

"How is it that the hawk sits on your hand?" I asked.

"I take a hawk from its nest and train it to hunt. When I have had it for two years, I let it go and train another. My ba ba taught me and his ba ba taught him." Ling saw the book in my hand. "You have not read the book already?"

"No, the book is only an excuse. I have a great worry." Quickly the words tumbled out. It was a relief to tell someone else of Quan's problems, for they had been too much for me to carry alone.

Ling listened closely to my story. "How could Quan ask such a thing of you? It is impossible."

"No," I said. "I must go or Quan will stay in jail forever. Han Na has been so kind to me, I must do what I can for her son."

"I will go," Ling said. "This is a time of year when the trees don't need me. The making of the new land can wait."

I shook my head. "A young man like yourself without a residence permit would be as likely to be arrested as Quan, and there is not enough money for two fines. I'll dress like a young girl. No one will suspect me. It is something that I must do. I came to you for help in doing it."

Ling had many arguments against my going to Shanghai, but at last he saw that I meant to make the trip. "I'll go into the village in the morning and see when the train goes to Shanghai and how much a ticket will be," he said. "Shanghai itself is another matter." He looked thoughtful. "I'll come to your house to tell you what I've found." He gave me a searching look. "Quan is lucky to have such a good friend," he said, as if he were asking a question.

Quickly I told him, "It is not my friendship for Quan but my friendship for Han Na. I would do anything for her happiness."

At that moment the hawk returned, a pheasant in its beak. The hawk landed on Ling's outstretched hand, and Ling took the struggling bird from the hawk and wrung its neck. "Here, take it for Han Na's supper."

I shook my head. The hawk had been very beautiful in its soaring, but my feelings were all for the pheasant. Misfortune had swept down upon me like the hawk and now, like the pheasant, I must struggle. I did not want the unfortunate bird to remind me of failure.

I had the night to get through. The moment I lay down, my head filled with my troubles, and I could hardly breathe. The night, which had always seemed quiet, was now full of noises. An owl screeched, frightening the roosting chickens. A cricket found its way into the room, and I could not close my eyes for waiting for its next chirp. I thought of how my ye ye had said, "At night the crickets sing away the darkness," but this night the darkness seemed never to end. I went over and over Quan's words hoping to find some way to get around them. Sleep would have been a comfort, but my eyes would not close. I felt as if the whole world were smooth with sleep and I was a great bump. When the morning came, I nearly cried with relief until I thought of what lay ahead.

It was the middle of the morning when Ling appeared in our field. He greeted Han Na courteously. "I stopped on my way home from the village," he said, "with the thought that if Chu Ju could be spared from her work, she might wish to walk partway to the hill with me. The morning is pleasant."

Han Na stared a little but after a moment said, "Yes, of course, if Chu Ju wishes." She smiled knowingly at me. "Be back for our noon rice."

When we were a little distance, Ling said, "Are you still set on making such a trip?"

"Yes, I must go at once." It was not only that I was anxious to get Quan from the detention center, but I was so upset with worrying about the trip, it would only be the leaving that would end my misery.

"Well then, if it must be. The train that goes to Shanghai stops in the village at six o'clock this evening. You will be in Shanghai at noon tomorrow. You must buy a ticket for a hard seat, that is the cheapest, and as you said, you must make yourself look like a child, for the fare will be cheaper yet. Take some food with you. And here, for only a few yuan I found this pamphlet with a map of Shanghai. See, right here in the train station there is the underground train that takes you anywhere in the city. There is no need to wander the streets. And Chu Ju, should anyone ask, you must have a story in your head of why you are there, but the story must not say that you carry money with you. Tell no one that."

Ling gave me a worried look. "Chu Ju, I wish

you would let me go in your place."

I shook my head. "And if they kept you as well? No. It must be me. If I am to go tonight, I must hurry home and prepare." I took hold of his hand and thanked him for his help. A moment later I was running back to Han Na.

I was out of breath when I reached her. "Han Na," I said, "I must go to see my parents. I leave today."

Han Na's eyebrows flew up. "What, today! What has Ling said to you? I like the boy, but this suddenness is foolish. You are only sixteen. Wait a little until you have thought on it."

I was happy to let her believe Ling was the excuse for my hurrying away, for what other excuse could I offer? "I promise I will take no foolish action with Ling, but I must see my parents."

Han Na saw my determination. "If you must go, I cannot keep you here, but Chu Ju, I wish you would wait a bit."

I shook my head. "It is only for a few days. I promise to come right back. It is the quiet time of year for the vegetables." Han Na sighed and said nothing more.

The worst part was yet to come. "How will you go?" she asked.

"By the bus from the village," I lied, knowing that it was just the first lie I would have to tell.

"You must have some money for the trip," she said. Han Na got out the package of money that Quan had sent and gave me twenty yuan.

I felt my face grow hot as I took them and thanked Han Na, knowing that I would have to find a way to take all the money before I left.

The way came when Han Na went out to pick some radishes for me to take on my journey. The money when I took it was like a poisonous scorpion in my hand. It would have been no surprise if it had bitten me. Quickly I put it inside my jacket in a little pocket I had hastily made. I copied the address in Quan's letter. A moment later Han Na returned with the radishes, which she wrapped along with rice cakes and two hard-boiled eggs.

In the early afternoon I said my farewell to Han Na, unable to leave without shedding tears. Han Na cried as well. "With Quan away, you have been both a daughter and a son to me. This house is your house. Promise me you will come back."

I promised, but inside I wondered if there would be any returning from such a journey. At last I set off for the village, the money burning the place next to my heart where it lay. Several times I turned around to wave to Han Na, who stood there watching me, her hand shading her eyes from the bright sun. Then I turned a bend in the road, and when I looked back, Han Na's house was no longer there.

eight

To make myself look as much as possible like a young girl, I tied my hair into two untidy ponytails and put on a shirt that hid the part of my body that had become a woman. On the way to the village I made up my story. I would say that I was being sent to Shanghai to look after my grandmother, who was not well.

When I reached the station, I was afraid I would not be able to open my mouth to buy so strange a thing as a round-trip ticket to Shanghai, but I had practiced the words, and when I needed them the words appeared. The train came with many cars and many doors. I stood there puzzled as to which door I should enter and terrified that the train might take off without me. At last I followed a woman into a car crowded with passengers. She pushed her way onto a bench, finding room where there had been no room before.

I looked to see if there was somewhere else to sit, but there was no space and no one willing to make one. I stood grasping a pole to steady myself and watched as mile after mile took me farther from Han Na and closer to Shanghai. The train stopped and a man got out of the car, but when he had left, his space quickly filled up. Still I knew the space had been there and I pushed my way until it opened again. After I was seated, I felt a little better and even began to look out of the window with interest.

We crossed the river and I looked for Wu's fishing boat, but the bridge was high, the boats small, and one fishing boat looked like another. As the train rushed along, I thought of the map of China that had stretched across our wall at school. At last I was seeing China, and in spite of my worry over what was to come, I was excited and looked with amazement at the kilometers of countryside and the sizes of the towns through which we passed. I dreaded my arrival at Shanghai and wished I could stay on the train forever, watching as more and more wonders flew by.

After a little while the passengers brought out their dinners. The man next to me unwrapped a feast with little packages of this and that. The packages slid onto my lap and spilled onto the lap of the woman on his other side. There was much garlic on everything. He ate his way greedily through each package until nothing was left but a few small bones and the paper, which he threw on the floor. When he was finished and there was room, I opened my own small supper, but after watching his greed and with my nervousness over the trip, I hardly touched what Han Na had packed for me. I began to wrap the food up again when the man, who had been watching me, said, "If you are not going to eat your dinner, so that it should not be wasted, I will eat it." And before I could answer, he had snatched it from me.

The night was long. The bench was hard, and because of the darkness there were no sights to see. I was hungry and wished for the rest of my dinner. The man next to me with his full belly slept soundly, often on my shoulder, the smell of garlic all around me, and I thought of the silkworms and how they would have hated to have a man with such a smell beside them, and I wished Jong were there to chase him away.

When morning came, we were traveling through rice paddies. The rice in the paddies was green and tall. We were so far south now that instead of winter vegetables the farmers could have two crops of rice—I had even heard that three crops were possible. It was warm and close in the car, but when the windows were opened to let in a little air, soot and bugs flew in as well. It began to feel as if I would spend the rest of my life hurtling along in the train.

As the train grew closer to the great city, there were no spaces on the benches for the passengers who boarded the train. The new passengers stood swaying in the aisles, bumping against one another. An older woman stood guarding a basket she had placed on the floor between her feet leaving her hands free to hang on to an edge of the bench on which I was sitting. She was old and tired looking, but patient, as if she had been shaken and rocked back and forth in trains all of her life. I signaled to her that she should take my seat, not wanting to get up until she was ready to sit down, for fear my small space would disappear. With a weak smile she settled into the space, clutching her basket to her.

"You are going to Shanghai?" she asked.

I nodded.

She said nothing more but looked at me from time to time as if she were trying to guess what I was doing by myself. At last, in a voice so quiet I could hardly hear her, she asked, "You are traveling alone?"

My story was ready. "Yes, my grandmother is unwell and I am on my way to her."

"She is fortunate to have such a kind granddaughter. Tell her for me you have done a kindness to an old woman."

I smiled at her and hated my lie.

From the train windows there were frightening sights. A huge city was unfolding, one ugly thing after another. Great square cement buildings, some with windows that showed people must live in them, others with no windows where unfortunate people must work, and perhaps where Quan had worked. I thought of Ling's wish to live where you might look out at the paddies and the hills.

The streets were crowded with bicycles and carts and taxis and more automobiles than I had thought possible. You could not see the sidewalks for the crowds of people. My heart sank. Was I to walk out into such a city among millions of people and find Quan? I took out my piece of paper. Before, the address had been a place; now it was only a single drop of water in an ocean. People began to collect their bags and baskets, ready to leave the train. Though I blinked my eyes, I could not keep back the tears. How was I to leave the train? I began to hate Quan for his stubbornness in going to such a city. I felt for my round-trip ticket, thinking I might stay on the train as it turned around and in less than two days be back with Han Na.

I saw the woman was still watching me, and

though no one else in the crowded car had noticed my unhappiness, for doubtless they had their own unhappiness at having to go to such a city, the old woman had noticed.

She stood up and put a gentle hand on my shoulder. In a soft voice she said, "Let me help you."

I was desperate for such help. I showed her my scrap of paper. "This is my grandmother's address," I said. "Could you tell me how to get there?"

When she saw the address she gasped, hastily handing the paper back as if it were a poisonous snake.

"Everyone in the city knows that address," she whispered. "I can tell you how to go there, but it is no place for a young girl. Can your grandmother be in a detention center?"

I felt I must take a chance, for in minutes we would leave the train and I would be alone in the city. I told Quan's story.

"You are as good-hearted as I believed," the woman said, "but you are foolish as well to take such a thing on yourself. Yet what kindhearted person does not have some foolishness about him? There is an underground train that will take you there. You can board it from the station. I will show it to you. I would go with you myself, but I am on my own sad errand. My daughter's child is sick, yet if my daughter does not leave her child each day to go to work, the two of them will starve. I am here to stay with the child."

"And the child's father?" I asked.

In yet a quieter voice the woman said, "He is in a reeducation center, and no amount of money will pay his way to freedom."

"What did he do?" I asked. I thought of a great theft or a cruel murder.

The woman's kind face became bitter. She looked about, but the other passengers in the crowded car were busy with their belongings. "He spoke the truth," she whispered. "It was a truth the government did not want to hear."

Before I could ask another question, the train came to a jerking halt and we were all thrown against one another. The woman took my arm, and together we left the train. The station was so huge, and the crowd so great, I had no time to ask why a man should be held captive for speaking the truth or what that truth might be, but I thought of Ling with his books that spoke the truth and I trembled for him.

There were farmers and elegant city people, soldiers, and even families cooking food and sleeping on mattresses as if the station were their home. The woman and I pushed through the crowds until we came to a machine with a line behind it. "You will need three yuan," she said. I gave her the amount. When our turn came, she put the money into the machine, and for the money she received two slips of paper from the machine's mouth.

"Through there," she said. "You must get on the train with this sign." She pointed to a name on the map that was posted on the wall. "And you must get off when you see this sign. Count the stops. Here is your train now." She gave me a little push toward the train and left me.

This train was more crowded than the train I had just left. There was no question of a seat, so I stood grasping an overhead handle for balance and peering at the station signs as we came to them. Unlike the first train, where there was something to see from the windows, the underground sped along through a tunnel of darkness. At each station there was the surprise of learning the world was still there.

After many stops we came to the station the

woman had named. I pushed my way out and climbed a stairway onto a street in the center of the city. I had been cast out into the midst of speeding automobiles, tall buildings, and thousands of people. I had no idea of where to go next. In our village if someone stood in the middle of the road, not knowing whether to turn this way or that, someone would stop to help. Here in the city it was like the trays of worms that cared only for the chewing of their leaves and nothing for the other worms. Hundreds of people passed me as if I were only a small pebble to be pushed aside or trod upon. Even the air was unfriendly. It had the smell of rotten eggs, and I dared not breathe deeply.

A great bus stopped, and when the door of the bus opened fifty *waiguoren* climbed out. Of course I knew *waiguoren* came to see the beauties of China, but why were they not taken to the paddies and the hills, where they could breathe the air and see something pleasant? I was sorry for them. One of the *waiguoren* smiled at me and, pointing the camera at me, took my picture. I was so startled, I could only stand there as the *waiguoren* hurried away, following a woman holding a little banner.

Squeezed into one of the large buildings was a small noodle shop. I was weak with hunger. I did not want to spend a single yuan of Quan's money, but I thought with a few noodles in my stomach my courage would return. The man in the noodle shop smiled at me, filling my bowl to the top. Here was a surprise, a smile and generosity in the city. I watched him as I ate my noodles. There were generous portions and smiles for everyone. I stood in line again. He laughed. "What, more noodles?"

I shook my head and held out my scrap of paper. He glanced at the address and reached for my bowl.

"Two streets down," he said. "The building

with the police at the door." He began to refill my bowl.

"No," I said. "I have no more money."

"These are free noodles," he said. "They were waiting just for you."

The free noodles were as tasty as the ones I had paid for, and because of the man's kindness I walked out into the street with more courage. The building with the police was as he described. Many people were going in and also coming out. No question was asked of me at the door. Inside, long benches were filled with unhappy-looking people. I whispered a question to one of them, and she pointed to the desk. At the desk a young woman peered up at me. Her hair must have been cut with the help of a ruler and her clothes were also neat and unbecoming. She asked question after question in a loud voice, as if I might be too stupid to answer unless I was shaken out of my senses by shouting. "What is his name? Where is his village? When did he come here? What was his address in Shanghai?"

Quan's record was discovered. "You must pay ninety yuan," she said.

Never had I been so happy, for I had that many yuan and a little more left besides to take back to Han Na. I handed the loud woman the money.

"Wait over there." She pointed to a bench.

An hour passed and then another hour. Every so often someone would be called to the desk or a door would open and prisoners would come out with uncertain steps, their eyes blinking, a startled look on their faces as if they had been closed into some dark place where no light came. I thought of the woman's son-in-law whose freedom could not be purchased. He had been brave indeed to speak the truth.

At last Quan came through the door. He looked many years older and put his hand on my shoulder as if he needed my support. The moment we were out of the building, he led me around the first corner and away from the sight of the police.

"Quan," I said, "there is enough left for your railway ticket and a little besides."

"No, no. I am not going back."

"But you have no residence permit. You will be arrested again, and there are not enough yuan to free you a second time. Anyhow, I would not make a second trip for anything."

"I'm wiser now," Quan said. "They won't catch me again. I have no wish to go back to the country. There is nothing there. Here there is money to earn and something happening every minute."

"What good is the money if it must go to fines? What good is something happening if what is happening is bad?"

But Quan was stubborn. "It was good of you to make the trip, but I will stay here. When do you mean to go back?"

"This minute."

"No. We will find a late train. It will soon be

dark, and you must see Shanghai by night."

Though I protested, he would have it his way. Quan hurried through the streets, each one as familiar to him as our village streets were to me. Yet I saw that he took me along back streets and often looked over his shoulder. That is the way he will live, I thought, as if he were a hunted animal.

"Quan," I said, "the woman who showed me how to find you has a son-in-law who was arrested for speaking the truth, and she cannot get him out."

"He is a fool to risk arrest for speaking the truth."

"But Quan, you risked being arrested for money."

"That is different," Quan said.

I thought it was indeed different, and I liked Quan less.

Though I liked him less, I could see how much pleasure Quan took in showing Shanghai to me. He led me into a park where trees grew and there was a pond where children were feeding giant carp as large as pigs.

All the while, Quan filled my ear with bragging about the city. It was as if the city were someone with whom he had fallen in love. "Shanghai has fourteen million people. Imagine that." He smiled proudly as if he had met each person, but I trembled at such a number.

Nearby was a bazaar with a thousand things I had never seen the likes of: cages of crickets, some cages labeled FIGHTING CRICKETS and some labeled SINGING CRICKETS. There were things to put here and there in a house, and elegant clothes to wear. When I lingered over a silk scarf, thinking of the worms, Quan said, "Spend a few of the yuan that are left on the scarf. It is payment for making the trip."

I shook my head. "No payment is needed," I said. "I did it for Han Na." Certainly I had not done it for Quan. "But there is one thing. I want to send a letter."

Quan bought me paper and a stamp, borrowing a pen from the shop owner. At last I wrote to my parents, for they would look at the postmark, and seeing it was from a city of many millions, they would not think of looking for me.

Dear Ma Ma and Ba Ba,

> *I should have written long ago. I am well and happy where I am. I have all the food I wish and I live in the home of an honorable woman who cares for me. I have a bit of land to work that is a rice paddy in the summer and a field of vegetables in the winter. The crops thrive. If you have a son now, you need not worry that I will return. Kiss and hug Hua for me.*
>
> > *Your daughter, Chu Ju*

It was growing dark, and all around us the buildings began to light up as if they were gigantic fireflies. All the automobiles in the world circled above us on a road that seemed to hang from the heavens. Ahead of us was a river.

"The Huangpu," Quan said, and there was deep pleasure in his voice. "You must see the Waitan, the walkway along the river. It is the most beautiful walkway in the world."

Along the walkway were great buildings and hotels and parks and music playing and the delicious smells of food. On the river were hundreds of illuminated junks and barges hung with lanterns, so the Huangpu was a river of light. Crossing the river was a bridge strung with more lights and held up by a cobweb of iron threads. On the other side of the river was a great soaring tower that must have reached into heaven itself. It was lit with a thousand lights.

"That is the Minzhu, the *dian-shi* tower," Quan said. "It is called the Oriental Pearl. You can take an elevator to the very top. The building going up over there beyond the tower will be the tallest in all the world. It will be in that building that money matters all over Asia are decided." There was much pride in his voice. He might have put up the building himself, controlling all the money matters under his hand.

With such marvels I understood why Quan wished to stay in the city. It was not the money. The money he sent to Han Na. It did not matter to Quan if he worked all day at hard labor, if at night he could have all around him, and at no cost, sights such as this. Quan was surely in love with the city.

"When I return," I said, "I'll explain to your mother how beautiful the city is and how to you the beautiful city is worth the danger."

Quan grasped me roughly by the shoulder.

"You said that you told my mother that you were going to visit your family."

"Yes, but that was only so she would not worry that you were in jail and I was going alone to Shanghai. When I return I can tell the truth, for you are free and I will be home."

"No. You must promise to say nothing to my mother about coming here to Shanghai. You must keep telling the story of your visit to your family."

I stared at him. "How can I do that? After I left, Han Na must have seen that the yuan you sent were all gone. She will think I stole them."

"She will forgive you. You are a young girl, and she is fond of you and needs your help."

"No, she will never forgive me for stealing. I can't tell her such a lie."

"You must." Quan grasped my shoulder more tightly, until I cried out with pain. "Listen," he said, "would you have her die? That is what would happen if each morning she awoke to think I might be arrested again, in jail like that woman's son-in-law you told me about, perhaps forever. She could not live with such a worry."

I saw that Quan did not care what Han Na thought of me. He cared only that his mother should not learn he had been in a detention center. Yet how could I be sure he was not right, that such worries would kill Han Na and I would be the doing of it?

"Swear you will not tell her," Quan said.

At last I promised. Quan smiled and led me to a food stall. Using Han Na's money, he bought me dumplings with bits of duck, and chive pancakes, but I could not swallow them for worrying about what Han Na would think of me. Quan ate them for me. First my food went to the greedy man on the train and now to Quan. I thought bitterly of how many my misery had fed.

On the way to the station we passed a street filled with dancing people and blaring music. I stopped to look at the crowds, but Quan pulled me away. "Not for your eyes," he said. "Evil things go on there." I asked myself why Quan would want to live in such a city, with evil on streets he must pass each day.

When we reached the station, Quan did not wait with me for the train but hurried out into the night to enjoy his freedom in the firefly city he loved so much, while I boarded the train to return to Han Na and tell her my lies.

nine

As miserable as I was on the train, I did not want my journey to end. Rather than face Han Na, I would have been content to hurtle along forever. When the train reached our village, I had to force myself to get out. A soft rain was falling, but I hardly noticed it. As I walked from the village to Han Na's house, I was seeking an excuse to explain the taking of Quan's yuan. I had made a promise to Quan to keep his secret, but I did not see how I could face Han Na.

The sight of our crops shook me from my thoughts. No one had tended the land. I had been gone less than three days and already there were bugs on the squash, the weeds stretched higher than the radishes, and the sweet-potato vines were choking the cabbage heads. I had been dragging my feet, but after seeing how the crops had been neglected, I walked faster, afraid that Han Na was ill and had taken to her bed.

It would have been usual for me to walk through the door without knocking, for it was my house as well. Now I knocked. While I waited, the speech I had rehearsed flew away.

It was a new Han Na who opened the door. She was more stooped, her face thinner, her hair uncombed, her voice harsh. "Why did you come back? There is no place for you here and no money left for you to steal."

Her words were worse than a slap. "There is a little money left," I said, handing it to her. "I used only what I had to."

"If your family needed money, why did you not

come to me?" Han Na asked. "I would have given you all you asked for. Why did you steal what Quan worked so hard for? There is no place in my house for you."

"Han Na, the field is untended. Let me take care of it. I can sleep in the courtyard."

"The field is nothing to me. I was only keeping it for Quan, and for you if Quan did not return. I no longer care for the field."

My heart leaped at the words *and for you*. All the time we had been working and living together, Han Na had looked upon me as her own child, someone to whom she might give the land. I saw all that I had lost. I was crying now and, worse, so was Han Na. The truth shut inside me tore at my heart like a wild dog desperate to escape. Quan had warned me that learning he had been arrested would destroy his mother, but what could be worse than this? Just as the wild dog was ready to spring out, Han Na shut the door.

The journey with little sleep and much worry had tired me. I longed for a place to lie down. The courtyard was forbidden to me. I thought of Ling, but Han Na might have told Ling's parents, and Ling had promised to say nothing of the real purpose of my journey. The Zhangs would be no more willing than Han Na to have me in their home. I resigned myself to spending the night stretched out in some field in the rain and the darkness. "Even Ling's water buffalo has a roof over his head," I said to myself.

At the thought of the buffalo I began to climb the hill. It was nearly dark. I slipped from shadow to shadow, keeping well away from the Zhangs' house.

Three sides of the stable were closed to the weather. The stable roof was thatched with rice straw. I heard the buffalo moving about. Though his large size frightened me, I told myself that Ling said he was a great baby. I crept inside and was relieved to see that the brute was tethered to a stake, so a part of the stable was out of his reach. I sank down on a heap of rice straw, the smell and the warmth of the animal all about me. In a moment I was asleep.

When I awoke at the crow of the *gong-ji*s, I saw a line of light along the horizon. The water buffalo grunted and stirred in his sleep. Hastily I ran from the stable and climbed down the hill. Minutes later I was in Han Na's field, taming the sweet-potato vines, pulling weeds, and picking the bugs off the squash. I worked all morning, but Han Na never came. At noon I ate some radishes and raw cabbage, worried that even the little I put into my mouth was an act of theft.

By afternoon the field was as it should be, and I decided I must leave. It seemed that no sooner did

I find a house for myself than I had to run away, but what else could I do? Han Na had said there was no place for me. I had started on my way when something made me decide to say good-bye to Ling. I started up the hill. At one house I passed, I saw a family in its courtyard. How I longed to be part of such a family again, to have a house to live in, to sit at a table and lie on a bed and have someone with whom I could talk.

Ling was in the orchard, a pail of dirt on either end of his shoulder pole. The moment he saw me, he dropped the pole and ran to meet me. "Chu Ju! I am so glad to see you! What trouble you have made for yourself! My parents wanted Han Na to send the police after you, but she wouldn't do it. I kept my promise to say nothing, but now you will have told Han Na the truth. Is Quan free? Is he coming home?"

"No. He will never leave the city. It is like a

box of toys to him. He cares nothing for the land."

Ling shook his head. "And little for his mother."

"I think he cares for his mother. He sends her money, and he worried that she might learn what had happened to him." I was not fond of Quan—how could I be when he had made me so miserable?—but I saw that he had been caught by the city. If he had to choose between my misfortune and his mother's, why should he not choose mine?

"Chu Ju, you have told Han Na the truth?"

"No. I promised Quan I would say nothing about his being in the detention center. He will never come back, and Han Na would always be worrying that he would be arrested again. I can't do that to her. But Ling, she sent me away last night."

"Sent you away? It was raining. Where did you sleep?"

I couldn't help smiling. "I slept in your stable, beside the beast."

"Are you to spend the rest of your life with a water buffalo! Han Na loves Quan, but she loves you as well. When Quan left, she still worked in the paddy and cared for her garden. When you left, she shut herself into the house. I wanted to tell her the truth, but I had promised to say nothing until you returned. Now you are back and now I'm going to tell the truth." Ling started down the hill.

I ran after him. "Wait! What of my promise to Quan?"

"That was your promise. I made no such promise."

Ling marched down the hill. I had to run to keep up with him. The whole time, I was begging him to wait but he would not listen. He only marched on.

At Ling's loud knock Han Na opened her door and came out into the courtyard. When she saw me standing behind Ling, she said, "There is nothing to be said. It is better for you, Ling, to keep away from such a girl as that."

"Han Na," Ling said, "you must listen. You don't know the truth."

"There is no truth to learn from such a person," Han Na said. "All but a few of Quan's hard-earned yuan gone for who knows what foolishness. I would never have thought it of her."

In one breath Ling said, "The money went to pay a fine so Quan could be released from a detention center."

Han Na sunk down upon a chair and stared at us. "What are you saying? Quan is in Shanghai. Chu Ju went to her family."

"No," Ling insisted. "Quan was arrested because he had no residence permit. Chu Ju made the trip all the way to Shanghai to pay the fine with Quan's money."

Han Na looked at me. "Is that true?"

I nodded.

"But how is it you knew this, Chu Ju, and I didn't?"

"Quan put it in his letter and told me to say nothing. I didn't read that part to you. Quan said to take his yuan and bring them to the detention center in Shanghai so that his fine could be paid."

"You traveled to Shanghai by yourself? If such a thing was asked, Quan should have asked it of me."

I dared to put my hand on Han Na's, and a great weight was lifted when her hand grasped mine. "Han Na, Quan thought the trip would be too much for you."

"And would he have a girl of sixteen wander alone in such a city? Why didn't he come back with you? He will be arrested again in no time." I felt Han Na's hand tremble in mine.

"Quan knew you would worry. That's why he wouldn't let me tell you. But Han Na, Quan says he will not make the same mistake again."

"You must write him to come home."

"Quan will not come home. Han Na, let me tell you what the city is like for Quan. He knows every part of it as we know our paddy and as Ling knows his orchard. The city is not for me or for you or for Ling, but it is full of wonders and very beautiful by night. Quan sees only the beauty. He will never come back."

Ling said, "I'm going to tell my parents the truth. I'll stop back later. Before you ask Chu Ju more questions, Han Na, you should give her something to eat and let her clean herself. She smells like a water buffalo." Laughing, Ling hurried away.

Han Na quickly put a bowl of rice and some hard-boiled eggs before me. As she boiled water for tea, she said, "Eat first, and then you must tell me how you made such a trip and how my son is."

I told of the train trip and the woman who

helped me, saying nothing of how that woman's son-in-law had been arrested for speaking the truth. I told her of the underground train and the noodle shop and all the places Quan had taken me in the city.

There were tears in her eyes. "I see that I may never think of my son coming home." After a bit she was calmer. "Can you forgive me, Chu Ju? The words I said to you yesterday were terrible."

"But I deceived you," I said.

"It was Quan who deceived me. Now let us have nothing but truth between us. Tell me why you came here and why you were wandering about alone. Who are your family, and why are you separated from them?"

I wanted the truth between us as well. I told Han Na the story of my parents and my grandmother and of Hua. "I could not let them sell my sister."

Han Na groaned and took me in her arms. "Terrible, terrible. But Chu Ju, what must your mother and father be feeling? At least I know where Quan is. You must go to them and tell them that you will always have a home here."

I shook my head.

"I cannot make you, Chu Ju, but you must begin to think about it. The day must come."

I did begin to think of it. A great longing that I had put aside came over me. Even if there were a son now, if I went back just for a short time there would be no question of anyone discovering I was another daughter. I would come and go quickly. For nearly two years I had put such thoughts out of my head. I had said to myself that I would never return, that my family was lost to me forever. Once I began to think of returning, I could think of nothing else.

Still, the months went by and I did nothing further about such a visit. I worried about leaving Han

Na, for she grew a little weaker each day. She seldom went into the field now. When Quan's letters came, she hardly listened to the words he wrote. The money she put aside, no longer counting it. Once she said to me, "Chu Ju, the money is here when you are ready to make your journey home." She sighed. "I think you should make the journey, but I am afraid if you do, you won't come back to me."

"Han Na, this is my home now."

The last of the vegetables were harvested, and in March Ling brought the water buffalo and plowed our field.

"Here is your friend," Ling said. "He tells me he is lonesome at night for his old roommate."

After the field was plowed, Ling tied up the beast and together we sat beside the field in the shade of a clump of bamboo and ate our lunches, sharing our bean curd and pancakes and gratefully drinking our boiled water. The smell of the new earth was pleasant. A flock of black-and-white magpies explored the freshly plowed field for worms. The spring sky was a cloudless blue, and the bamboo leaves barely rustled in the still noon air.

I had never told Ling the story of my family. I told him now.

At first he listened as if I were telling some story out of a book, hardly believing in the tale. As I told the story, he saw the tears in my eyes and he believed.

"Chu Ju, how you must have loved your sister, but what might have happened to you could have been worse than what might have happened to your sister."

"No. I had my freedom. No one could have bought and sold me. I might have been hungry, but that would have been the worst of it."

"You were lucky. There are evil men who

kidnap grown women. But tell me, now that you are older will you go back and see your family?"

"I don't know. Han Na is my family now, and she needs me here. If I returned, my grandmother would say I was coming back to make trouble for them. Hua would still be in danger."

"Chu Ju, I cannot say I would have done as you did, but I cannot say what you did was wrong. Only how sad your parents must have been to lose such a girl as you."

ten

Still I put off my return, for April came and the planting of the new rice shoots, and after that Ling brought a pamphlet telling of how rice and fish might be grown together.

"The agricultural agent in the government office where I got you the pamphlet will give Han Na fingerlings to put in the paddy, and they will cost you nothing."

"Fingerlings?"

"Read the pamphlet. They are tiny fish that will grow while the rice grows. By the end of August you will have two crops to harvest."

I did not always believe in Ling's pamphlets,

for he had so many of them. Yet his orchard had grown from the pamphlets.

Han Na believed even less in the pamphlets. "I want nothing to do with the government," she said. "It was the government that put Quan in prison for moving about in his own country. It was the government that told your parents how many children they could have, so babies are sold like so many bags of rice."

"But Han Na, this is only the village agricultural agent. I have seen him at the teahouse with his birdcage. He whispers to his bird in such a sweet way. I am sure no trouble would come of it. In the pamphlet it says the fish eat not only the weeds but the mosquitoes as well. You know how you complain of the mosquitoes. Even if there were not enough fish to sell, there would be some for our meals."

"I will ask the Zhangs for advice," Han Na said.

The next day, though I begged her not to, she made the trip to the Zhangs' home, returning out of breath and sinking down upon a chair, pale and shaking with the exertion of climbing the hill. The Zhangs had seen how Ling's pear and plum and peach trees had grown from his pamphlets. They must have said as much to Han Na, for she reluctantly agreed to go with me to the agricultural agent and ask for the little fish. A nearby farmer was going into the village to buy straw and offered to take us there in his wagon and bring us back so that Han Na would not have to walk.

The government office was not like the detention center in Shanghai. There were no people sitting on long benches with sad faces, only the agricultural agent I had seen in the teahouse. The office was small and dusty, with pamphlets everywhere and with signs saying the pamphlets were free for the taking. Slogans were taped to the wall to encourage farmers to serve

China by increasing their crops: A GREAT CROP WILL MAKE A GREAT COUNTRY and THE FARMER IS THE HEART OF CHINA.

The agent asked courteously what we wanted, and Han Na said, "We have a small rice paddy and you have small fish. We would like your fish for our paddy."

The agent asked where the paddy was, and opening a large book, he turned the pages until he came to the place that showed Han Na's paddy along with all the other paddies nearby. When he saw the paddy was there, he nodded as if pleased with Han Na's request. "Yes, that is a good plan," he said. "New fingerlings came this morning." He went into a back room and returned with a basket in which there were plastic boxes full of water and hundreds of fish no more than a few millimeters in size. Laughing, he said, "When the fish are big, bring me one for my dinner."

Han Na bowed and thanked the officer, gingerly holding the basket as if the little fish might escape from the boxes and attack her. Quickly she handed the basket to me and made her escape from the office. When we were outside, she said, "How can such tiny fish come to anything? It is foolishness. Still, the plastic boxes and the basket will come in handy."

The fingerlings went into the rice paddy as the pamphlet instructed, and after that I had company as I weeded. The little fish swam between my toes and made small splashes as they rose to catch the mosquitoes. In no time they were as large as my finger. I brought Han Na to the paddy to see how they grew, and she shook her head in wonder, but she worried. "What if they eat the rice?"

"No," I promised. "The pamphlet says they eat only the grass." Still she did not believe in the pamphlet.

Now there were enemies to battle. The king-fishers came: the black-and-white ones with the feathery crests, the blue ones with the orange bills, and the ones with the fiery orange breasts. They hovered in the bamboo branches, and when my back was turned they dove into the water and flew away with fish in their bills. Even worse were the herons. There had always been herons in the pad-dies, for there were frogs and crawfish. Now they came more often. They stayed away in the daytime when I was there, but at twilight they waded through the paddies, their great, long legs moving so slowly that they hardly disturbed the water, their long, cruel beaks coming down mercilessly on the growing fish.

Still, many fish remained, and when August came, just as Ling had said, we had fish to sell.

"You must buy a net," Ling said.

"I have a net all ready," I told him. I had

bought sturdy string in the village, and with the skill I had learned from Yi Yi, I had made my own net and fastened it to a bamboo pole.

Ling was impressed. "You catch them and I'll clean them," he said.

I laughed. "I can clean the fish much faster than you."

It was true. For every fish that Ling cleaned, I cleaned two. Each day I caught enough fish to take into the village to sell, and each day I brought back money for Han Na. We had fish for dinner each night. Several of the fish were sent with Ling to the Zhangs, some of the fish we dried, and the largest fish I brought to the agent in the agricultural office.

There was no thought now of returning to my family, for Han Na had grown weak and kept to the house. At first I thought her illness was worry over Quan, but a letter came from Quan full of good news. Because of all the building in Shanghai and because of his skill as a stonemason, something he had learned from his ba ba, he had been given a residence permit. The threat of being arrested was over. Han Na smiled, but still the weakness grew. I urged her to see the village doctor, but she would not go to him.

"He can't give me a new heart."

Ling, who read the newspapers in the village, said that in some large cities new hearts were given.

Han Na was horrified. "Ah, and what if a cruel heart were put into my body? I would never take the chance."

It was on the day when the last of the rice had been harvested that two policemen came by our house. They were not the familiar village policemen. Han Na was inside, and I was in the courtyard threshing the rice grains we were keeping for ourselves. The sight of the policemen sent my heart racing. Perhaps Quan was in new trouble or they had discovered that I had run away. The policemen paused when they saw me. They looked to me like the herons, tall and thin, and treacherous, as if they were ready to pounce.

One of the herons said, "We are looking for the Zhangs' house and for Zhang Ling. Do you know him?" He smiled as he asked, but he was looking at me as if he were considering if I might make a meal.

"Zhang? No, I know of no Zhangs around here," I said, and went back to my threshing.

They rounded a corner and were out of sight. I flew up the hill to the Zhangs', taking a shortcut. Ling was cleaning out the stable and changing the beast's straw.

"Policemen are asking for you," I managed to get out. "I told them I didn't know who you are. Ling, what have you done?"

"It must be the books," he said. "I was careless in getting the last one, buying it from someone I did not know." He began pulling several of his books from his shelf and throwing them onto a pile of the beast's manure, shoveling the manure on top of the books. There were tears in his eyes. "They won't look there," he said in a grim voice. He turned to me. "Go back to your house at once. You told them you didn't know me. They mustn't find you here. And Chu Ju, thank you. You have saved me. Now, go, quickly."

I saw the policemen coming up the hill and hid behind some boulders until they entered the Zhangs' house. Then I fled to our courtyard and began to thresh again, all the while watching the path. It was an hour before the policemen marched down the path from the Zhangs'. Ling marched with them, but he did not look in my direction. My hands shook so, all the rice I had winnowed tumbled out of my basket and was lost on the stones of the courtyard.

Han Na had not been well and I did not dare to worry her. Instead, I ran again to the Zhangs' house and found Ling's ba ba and ma ma in the midst of upheaval. The neat rooms were turned upside down. Ling's ma ma was sitting in a chair sobbing.

"They have taken my son," she wailed.

Ling's ba ba tried to calm her. "They found nothing. They will soon see their mistake and return him."

I thought of the boy who had been arrested for speaking the truth but said nothing of my fears. "What happened?" I asked.

Ling's father said, "Two policemen came and accused Ling of having forbidden books, but though they turned the house upside down, they could find no such books. Still they insisted on questioning him. He is a good boy and only tends his orchard. I told them to look at his trees and see if he was a dangerous man."

I said what I could to comfort the Zhangs and left, stopping in the stable on the way. The pile of manure was untouched, and I patted the beast, grateful for the fine hiding place he had made.

All day I stayed in the courtyard, watching the path, but Ling did not return. At daybreak I was there again, still watching. I thought I might go into the village, for like everyone else I knew where the small jail was. But should the policemen see me, they would be suspicious, and that might make things worse for Ling. I could not worry Han Na with the story, and I was afraid to go back to the Zhangs, for the police might return there. I could only wait. Over and over I tried to think what books might be dangerous, over and over I thought of the woman's son-in-law arrested for speaking the truth. If Ling's books spoke the truth, maybe that was dangerous. Yet they had not found the books.

Han Na knew something was wrong. "You live on air, not eating your rice or fish."

"I'm just restless. I've finished the threshing, and most of the vegetables have been planted."

"Why can you not enjoy a little time to yourself? If you must do something, go and help Ling with his trees."

But I could not help Ling with his trees. "I'll go into the village and get more radish seeds. There is yet room for another row or two."

I hurried off, relieved to have some errand. The road to the village followed one paddy after another. Like ours, the paddies lay waiting for the first radish seeds to sprout. Now there was only brown earth, with no bright green to lift the spirits. A rat scurried by in a ditch, and magpies hovered on a light wind. In one paddy a *ma-que* was snatching newly sown seeds. I thought that I must make another scarecrow so that our seeds would not be stolen by the little hungry birds.

As I passed the paddies, the farmers at their hoeing looked up. Some who knew me waved an arm in greeting and I waved back. It was early September and still warm. I longed to roll up my sleeves, but it would have been unseemly to appear in the village like that.

I could hear the sounds of the village long before I reached it. The old men sat in the teahouse, many of them with their birdcages. The butcher slew the flies that hovered over his meat, while the chickens and ducks clucked and squawked away in their cages. There was a crowd of children lined up to watch the *dian-shi* in the store window. The locksmith was sharpening hoes, and the man in the noodle shop waved, waiting for me to stop by for my bowl of noodles. I shook my head and hurried on. As I turned into the street that led to the jail—for I could not keep away from it—I saw Ling.

I looked hastily around, but no policeman was in sight; Ling was all by himself hurrying along the road. I ran up to him. I wanted to fling my arms around him, but such a gesture would never do. Still, I could not keep my hands entirely from him, for I was not yet sure he was really there.

He looked quickly around and, taking my hand in his, began to pull me away from the village. I saw that his hair was uncombed and his clothes were wrinkled, as if he had slept in them. His glasses sat crookedly on his nose, the nosepiece broken and fastened with tape.

"They kept me overnight, asking again and again about my books, but they had not found them and there was nothing else against me. I told them of how I had made the orchard and begged them to talk to the agent in the village government office, who has helped me through his pamphlets. They did talk with him, and he told them I was just a farmer.

Still, they will keep an eye on me."

"How did they know about the books?"

"I send away for them and there are spies everywhere, even in the post office where the books are mailed. I have been foolish and have given my parents trouble and worry."

As we talked, we hurried along the uphill path toward Ling's house and I was out of breath. "Are you finished then with such books?" I managed to ask.

"I don't know. I hope the day will come when everyone can have books that tell the truth."

I told Ling, "When I traveled to Shanghai, I talked with a woman whose son-in-law was arrested and sent to a reeducation center because he spoke the truth. If you have books that speak the truth, isn't that just as dangerous?"

"Dangerous, yes, but it is the books I had that make us remember what has happened to such people as the man you speak of. Are we to forget them? It would make their arrests even worse."

There was no more time for talk. Ling's parents had seen us in the distance and were running toward us. I turned back to Han Na's house. It would have been unseemly for me to be at the Zhangs' at such a time. Behind me I could hear their happy cries. I was crying as well, but whether with relief or worry I could not say.

eleven

Once more Ling plowed the paddy and the rice was planted and the little fish swam about. I worried less about Ling, for there had been no more policemen. Ling and I had worn a path up and down the hill between our houses. After our work was through, we rested in the long twilights, chewing sunflower seeds and talking. Though we were together nearly every day, still there was always something new to say to each other. One evening while we sat in Han Na's bamboo grove, half hidden from sight, a pair of cranes dropped down onto the rice paddy. We were pleased, for cranes, which mate for life, are much admired for their faithfulness and considered good luck. The tall, long-legged, gray birds with their brown-tipped wings and slender white-striped throats began to call to each other in a kind of duet. Then began a courting dance. The one bird would fly up and flutter about, and then the other bird would leap about doing the same. After they flew away, we were silent, for each year there are fewer and fewer cranes. After a moment Ling smiled and said, "I will practice that dance, Chu Ju, if you will also," and our sadness left us as we laughed.

There was another sadness. Han Na's weakness had been increasing, but it had been so gradual that I had become used to her waning strength. Each day she did a bit less, and each day I undertook a bit more. With just the two of us and the two rooms, there was little to do in the house, so I thought nothing of the few tasks that fell to me, but on the first day of the fifth moon Han Na did not get up from her bed.

She would not eat the rice gruel I brought to her. She put it aside and asked me to sit with her. "Chu Ju, you are a farmer now. You see how the rice is sown in the spring and harvested in the fall; one follows the other, and the harvesting is as necessary as the sowing. I am coming to the end of my days, Chu Ju."

"No, Han Na," I cried. I hung on to her hand, which was as dry and light as a piece of paper. "We will find a doctor to make you better."

"The knowledge of a doctor will make no difference. I listen to my heart at night, and that is all the knowledge I need. I have been fortunate, Chu Ju. My hard times are long past. My husband loved the land and worked until he owned a bit of it. My son is safe, never mind that he is far away. He is happy where he is, and he has not forgotten me or shamed me. I would have given much to have him bring a wife and one day a grandchild to meet me, but there will be no time for that. I am content with what I have." She clasped my other hand. "It was a fortunate day, Chu Ju, when I saw you. Now you must write to Quan and tell him to come and see me. Tell him he must come at once."

I wrote the letter and we waited for Quan. One day followed another, and each day Han Na grew weaker. Though she was against it, I went to the village and gave the doctor money to come to the house.

"You must go to the hospital in the next village," he told her, "and you must do it sooner rather than later."

Han Na refused. Nor would she have needles or herbs.

"Han Na," I begged, "if you will not do it for yourself, do it for me."

Han Na only shook her head. Her gaze was

always on the door, waiting for Quan. I would have gone myself to drag Quan home from his beloved city, but I could not leave Han Na. It was nearly the end of the fifth moon when Quan came. He was tender with his mother and wept at her weakness, but he took no notice of the rice paddy and sent me to the village to buy him the Shanghai newspaper.

In the evening Han Na asked Quan to carry her out to the courtyard so that she could see how the rice was growing. "Quan," she asked, "could you not return and work the land? Chu Ju has added fish to the rice, so the paddy is as good as a lake. It is a wonderful thing."

"No, Ma Ma. I am happy where I am. I was never meant to be a farmer. There is nothing about putting my hands into the earth that raises my spirits. I am a builder. The choosing and lifting and placing of the stones is what gives me pleasure, that and the great city."

"But when I am gone, Quan, what will become of the land? And the money you have sent—it is all there. We have not spent a penny."

"I will take the money I have sent you. It may be that it will let me marry. Do what you want with the land."

"Then it must be Chu Ju's. She has planted the rice and tended it as it should be tended. Even the little fishes have thrived under her hand. Chu Ju will make enough money from the crops to pay the rent fees and the taxes. She is eighteen now, and if she marries, her lease on the land will be her dowry.

"But Chu Ju," Han Na said to me, and took my hand in hers, "do not think that the land is payment for caring for me. There can be no payment for that. Where there was your love, there is only my love. And Chu Ju, you must promise me to see your parents. Look how I waited for Quan. Your ma ma waits for you as well. Promise me you will see her."

I promised.

In two days' time Quan was ready to return to the city, but Han Na said, "Wait a few days and you will not have to make the return trip."

Quan was horrified. "Ma Ma, are you to hurry with your dying so that I need not make a second trip? I am only going because I am sure you will soon be well." No one believed Quan's words, least of all Quan.

Han Na had only a little strength, but with the little she had, she mended the worn places on her best jacket. Neither she nor I said a word, yet we both knew why the mending was carried on.

On the day Quan was to return to the city, Han Na died. I saw that Quan was ashamed of his tears, and leaving Quan with his ma ma, I took my tears out to the paddy. I thought back to the day when I had first seen Han Na in the paddy, working along-side Quan. She had asked no questions of me but had taken me into her house and given me a home. Her house had become my house. What would my life be without her? I had given up my own family, and now the only family I knew was gone.

A soft wind rippled the rice, making green waves on a green ocean. Beyond our paddy were endless paddies, endless green oceans whose harvest would one day fill a million bowls. In the distance a heron stalked a frog, piercing it with its sharp beak, throwing it up in the air, and swallowing it with one gulp. With all the plenty there was cruelty. There had been Han Na's love as wide as a *hai* and now she was gone, snatched from me forever. I hunched down and, covering my face with my hands, cried until there were no tears left.

Ling's ma ma came bringing food and comfort. Together we readied Han Na in the mended jacket and covered her face with a bit of silk cloth. Though I thought it superstition, I said nothing when Ling's ma ma bound Han Na's feet together with string to keep her from moving about in the coffin should she become possessed by evil spirits. Ling's ma ma and I fashioned a wreath of white paper and bamboo, while Quan wrote out stories of Han Na's life on strips of white paper, which he hung at the entrance to the house.

A diviner was called and a date set for the funeral. I knew that it might be as long as a month before a date was chosen for the burial. Perhaps Quan was generous with the diviner, for the diviner found the very next day to be an auspicious one.

A coffin was purchased. A Taoist priest was summoned from the village to chant a sutra for the dead and a musician came to play the *suona*, whose mournful music tore at my heart. An empty chair was carried in the procession so that Han Na's spirit might join it and not stay behind to haunt the living, though I would have given much to have her about me.

Along with the other women I walked at the front of the procession. Ling's ma ma had instructed me that as the "daughter" of the house I had a duty to cry and wail, which would help to destroy the barriers Han Na might meet with as she started her long journey through the many realms of the Underworld. I had no need to be prompted, for the crying and wailing came from my heart.

When we returned home, Quan had the priest kindle a small fire. Before those of us in the procession could enter Han Na's house, we had to jump across the fire so that any evil spirits remaining from the death of Han Na would be left behind.

In all he did Quan honored Han Na, yet I could see that Quan was eager to return to Shanghai as soon as the funeral was over. "There is nothing more I can do here, and every day I am away, there is the chance that my job will be gone. Of the money I have sent, I will leave some yuan to carry you until the harvest. Unless, Chu Ju, you wish to share it all with me?"

"Share it?" I asked, puzzled. "It is yours, Quan. You are generous to give me the land. You might have sold the lease and taken the money. I am no blood relation to you."

"It was my mother's wish, and I could not go against that. Had you not stayed with her, I would never have been able to leave her and go to the city. When I was here, each day in the paddy was like a prison. But Chu Ju, that is not what I am speaking of. You could sell the lease and come with me to Shanghai. With the money of mine that Ma Ma saved and the money from the land, we could marry and find a small room of our own."

I stared at Quan in amazement.

"I know I am older than you are, Chu Ju, but I am a hard worker and it would be a great thing to live in such a city. You are clever and would have no trouble finding work. I have watched you since I have been here. You would make just the kind of wife I wish for."

I thought of the city at night with all its lights. I thought of cinemas, and stores with the silk scarves and with everything one could want. I thought also of living in one room, in one of the high buildings. I thought of the rush of people and cars and trolleys and the way when you went from place to place there was no path with paddies and bamboo groves but only a dark tunnel that shot you like a bullet from one stop to another.

"You are kind, Quan, but I would die in the city like a plant stuck into a pot of stones with no water or earth." I said nothing of Ling.

Quan looked disappointed but not surprised.

"Then we must go to the government office and register the lease in your name. You are eighteen now, and there will be no trouble."

The official at the government office frowned at Quan. "You are giving the lease for the land over to this young girl?"

Quan produced a letter that Han Na had had a scribe write for her and that she had signed with her mark. "It is all here. Chu Ju is to get the land, all five *mu*. We have the money for the fee, and she can pay the taxes when they are due as well as anyone else."

The official looked at me and Quan and then at the money Quan had given for the fee to transfer the land. At first I thought he would say no. Instead he said, "This transfer of lease is irregular and will cause me much extra work." He looked at Quan.

After a moment Quan said, "I am sorry for the

extra work. Let me increase the fee to make up for it." He put down more yuan, which the official swept up as quickly as the heron snatched the frog. The papers were completed and a seal put on them. Quan handed them to me and led me out of the office.

"I will wait in the tea shop for the train." He took my hand. "It was a day of great fortune when you came to us. I am only sorry you will not go back to Shanghai with me." With that he hurried away, and I turned toward my land.

twelve

Each day I thought of my promise to Han Na to visit my family. The only time I could leave would be after the rice harvest and before the crops were planted. At the end of August the time came. I would take a bus to the river and the riverboat to our village. I remembered my ba ba's dislike of blue jeans, and I bought new trousers for the trip and a new shirt as well. Then, throwing all caution to the winds, I spent three yuan for a stuffed panda for Hua.

All was ready and everything planned, yet I could not take the first step. It had been like that when I had left my home, and now it was like that when I was to leave Han Na's house.

Ling said, "Chu Ju, think how pleased and relieved your family will be to see you. You have nothing to fear. Who could wish for a better daughter? They will be proud to hear you have your own land."

"But I ran away."

"They will understand. Perhaps there is a son now. Though how any son could make them happier than such a daughter as you there is no knowing." A worried look came over his face. "You will come back?"

"I would never leave my land," I said. "And my friends are here. How could I leave your parents, who have been so good to me?" I smiled. "And their son as well."

As the bus pulled away from the village, the last thing I saw from the window of the bus was Ling standing at the station waving. I closed my eyes, holding the memory to carry me in the days to come.

The bus passed near the worm farm and I longed to stop and see Ling Li, Song Su, and Jing, but I could not stop, for I had to return in time to get the crops planted. The riverboat carried me on the water, and I looked for Yi Yi and Wu and the boys. There were many fishing boats, but none of them was familiar.

At last we came to the village where I had grown up. I left the boat, checking carefully to see that my return tickets were in my bag. It was early evening and many of the stalls in the village were closed. The dentist and Ba Ba were not there, but I saw my old schoolmaster. I was ready to greet him but he hardly looked at me, passing me quickly. I hurried on, thinking it might be possible to visit my home and see my family from a distance without being recognized.

My old home and its plot of vegetables had grown large in my memory. Now, with it there before my eyes, it appeared small. I stood hidden beside the many branches of the banyan tree. What I saw seemed both as real and yet as unreal as the pictures I had seen on the *dian-shi* screen in the window of the store. There was Nai Nai, older and frailer, sitting with Ba Ba at the table in the courtyard. Ma Ma held Hua in her arms. No. It could not be Hua, for the baby in her arms was only a few months old. A child ran out of the house and climbed onto Ba Ba's lap, and I saw that it was Hua. The terrible worry I had had all these years disappeared. My sister was safe.

Perhaps the new baby was a boy. I could see no place for myself and resolved to leave now, saying nothing. Later I would send a letter telling all that had happened to me. Yet in spite of my resolve to run away again, I drew closer. I might just say a word or two, ask directions as if I were a stranger, and not be recognized. My heart pounding, my legs weak, I stepped away from the shadow of the tree.

Ma Ma looked up and saw me. She thrust the baby into Nai Nai's arms and ran toward me. "Chu Ju! Chu Ju!" I felt the familiar softness as her arms enclosed me and smelled the familiar fragrance of the many herbs she gathered and preserved for Ba Ba. "Oh, Chu Ju, how could you have left us? Every day has been a torture worrying about you."

Ba Ba hurried toward me as well. He took my hands. "Chu Ju, your leaving us was a bitter thing. But let me look at you. The little girl is gone. You are a young woman now and comely."

Nai Nai was staring at me over the baby in her arms. I could not tell whether her eyes were bleary with age or whether tears lay in them. "How well you are dressed," she said. There was suspicion in her voice.

Hua, for I knew it was my sister, stood apart, staring at me, her thumb in her mouth. I knelt down and drew her to me. "Hua," I asked, "do you remember me? I am Chu Ju, your sister."

I took the panda bear from my bag and handed it to her. "I brought you a present."

Hua grinned and looked up to Ma Ma as if asking permission. Ma Ma nodded, and Hua reached for the bear, hugging it to her.

I was sorry I had not brought something for the new baby. "What is the new baby's name?" I asked.

"She is called Nu Hai," Nai Nai said. "Nothing else is needed."

Nu Hai, Girl, a name given with no great thought or hope.

"You must be hungry," Ma Ma said. "Come and sit down and let me get you tea and a little something with it."

Ma Ma brought out a hard-boiled egg and flat-cakes and my favorite pickles. The tea came in the familiar blue bowls I had drunk from so many times.

Watching me, Ma Ma said, "Every day I wondered, Where is Chu Ju this day? and even Where is Chu Ju this moment?"

Ba Ba said, "When I read your note, Chu Ju, I said it was all my doing. If there had been no talk of sending Hua away, we would still have our Chu Ju. In our desire for a son, we lost a daughter." He sighed. "Now we have another daughter, but this one stays, though I will never live to see a son."

When the table had been cleared, Ba Ba said, "Now, Chu Ju, you must tell us where you have been."

"From the moment you left," Ma Ma said. "Leave nothing out. I went with you on your journey, but I have no picture of it."

Hua climbed onto my lap, clutching her panda, anxious for a story with no thought that the story began with her.

With every sentence there were questions.

"But why did you think of going to the river?" Ba Ba asked.

"How could you deal with the insides of so many fish?" Ma Ma wanted to know.

"Worms!" Hua giggled. "You tickled the worms with a feather?"

"There can be little money in the tickling of worms," Nai Nai said. "How is it you have money to come back here? We want no thief in our house."

And so I told about Han Na's house.

When I had finished my story, Ma Ma said, "How I wish the good woman had lived so that I might go on my knees to thank her for her kindness to my daughter."

"You went to Shanghai by yourself?" Ba Ba

asked. "That is such a dangerous place."

"And now that your Han Na is dead," Nai Nai said, "I suppose this Quan has turned you out, and you come back here like a whipped dog with its tail between its legs."

"No indeed," I protested. "It is not like that at all. Han Na left me the lease for her land and Quan took me himself to the village registrar. The lease is mine. It is all recorded. I go back tomorrow to plant the vegetables."

"No!" Ma Ma cried, grasping my sleeve as if she meant to hold me there. "It is impossible that you should leave so soon. I just have my daughter back with me, and am I to lose her?"

But Ba Ba only asked, "This land belongs to you? How much land is there?"

When I told him, his eyes opened very wide, as if he saw before him the green rice plants rippling in the wind. I could tell that the idea of having even so little a piece of land was a great thing for Ba Ba. As I described the plowing of the land and planting of the rice, Ba Ba's face lit up as if he, too, were planting and harvesting. "And fish," I said. "I plant fish with the rice and they grow with the rice so that I have a double harvest."

Nai Nai gave a little bark of a laugh. "Now I am more sure than ever that you are telling us a tale. Fish in the rice paddy? That can't be."

"It can be," Ba Ba said. "I have heard of such things."

"With Han Na gone," Ma Ma said, "you will be alone."

I told them of the Zhangs' kindness, and because I wished to bring his name into our family, I told them of Ling and how he and the beast plowed my land and the cleverness of his orchard.

Ba Ba nodded his head as I described the orchard. "That is a wise choice. I see in the village how much people will give for a fine peach or juicy plum."

As I spoke of Ling, Ma Ma watched me. Now she smiled. "This son of your friend has an orchard and his family have a water buffalo? They must be well off. Is this Ling a good son?"

My face was burning. "Yes," I said. "And a good friend." I said no word of his dangerous books that told the truth.

"Ah," Ma Ma said, and nodded with satisfaction.

"I have been thinking," I said. "If the rice and fish do well this year, I could save my money and in a year or so send the fare for the boat and bus. Then you could see my land."

Nai Nai had been watching me. Now she said, "Why don't you sell the lease to your land and come here? You are grown now, and we could pass you off as a cousin. Then if there is a son, we would have the money for a fine."

Ma Ma said, "I am too old for another child. There will be no son, and who would not be satisfied with a daughter like Chu Ju?"

Ba Ba said, "Yes, sell your land and come back, and we will buy land here." There was eagerness, even hunger in his voice.

For a moment I thought of such a thing, but I saw it could not be done. "The land was left to me by Han Na, who wanted me to care for it. If I were to give it up, the money should go to Quan." Though I longed to stay close to Ma Ma, I saw my land before me as clearly as if it were there. I knew every furrow and every bit of rich earth. Who would care for the rice and the fish as I would? And was I to say good-bye to Ling forever? I knew something else. If I were to give the money to Ba Ba, it would be Ba Ba's land to do with as he pleased.

"You are a selfish girl," Nai Nai said, "to care so little for your family."

"I care for my family," I said, "and if money is needed, I will be thrifty and send all I can, but I am going to return tomorrow."

After our rice Hua took me by the hand. "Chu Ju," she said, "come and see the little chicks."

There in the chicken yard were three newly hatched chickens. Hua squatted down beside them and stared fondly at them, gently touching their soft yellow down. As I watched her, I promised myself that any money I gave would go for Hua's and Nu Hai's schooling, as much schooling as they wanted. I could live on very little. There would be no further new clothes. I would make whatever sacrifice was needed. Should I marry Ling, I was sure he would understand. Learning meant much to him, and hadn't he been quick to give me a book to read; hadn't he risked much for books? I did not believe that he would begrudge me any money I sent to my sisters.

Nai Nai must have read my mind, for she said,

"Though I said it would be a waste, your ba ba spent good money on educating you. There is no money to waste on schooling for your sisters." She gave me a sly look.

"I will find the money," I dared to say to her. "The learning was not wasted on me." I thought of the letter I had written to the orphanage and the reading of Quan's letters and the book I shared with Ling.

The following morning, when it was time to leave, the good-byes of Ba Ba and Nai Nai were stiff and formal. Ma Ma clung to me begging me not to leave. Hua, too, clung to me, and for a moment Han Na's house seemed so far I could not see it, but then it came back into my head, and promising to return, I hurried off, looking back only once.

It was still daylight when I reached the house that had been Han Na's and was now mine.

Though I was tired from the long trip, and though the memory of Ma Ma's sad farewells stayed with me, I went at once to the little seeds and began to drop them into the warm earth. Soon the green shoots would push up, and in time there would be the harvest and then another spring and the planting of the rice and the little fish swimming about. When I paused in my planting to look up toward the hills, I saw Ling hurrying toward me, a great smile on his face.

glossary

ba ba: father

budui: wrong, incorrect

cha hukou: the checking of residence permits

chi fan meiyou: literally, "Have you eaten yet?"
    Used as a greeting in China as we might say,
    "Hello."

dian-shi: television

feng shui: the art of finding the most auspicious
    placement for something

gong-ji: rooster

gu zheng: a stringed instrument resembling a lyre

hai: the sea

majiang: a game played with tiles

ma ma: mother

ma-que: a sparrowlike bird

mu: one sixth of an acre

nai nai: paternal grandmother

nu hai: girl

qing-ting: dragonfly

suona: woodwind instrument often played at funerals

waiguoren: foreign devils, a derogatory name for foreigners

ye ye: paternal grandfather

ying: eagle

yuan: about twelve cents in American currency

zai-jian: farewell

THE CHINESE NEW YEAR

The Chinese New Year is determined by the Chinese lunar calendar. It usually takes place in January or February and begins with the new moon.

A NOTE ON HUA'S AGE

Chinese babies are considered one year old when they are born, so one year after Hua was born, she was two years old.